"Together with his metaphysical imagination, his hard-earned understanding of science and technology, and his maturing skills as a delineator of character, his mastery of a distinctive prose style makes it impossible to regard Zebrowski as just another journeyman yarn-spinner...The strides he has made on a stylistic level—the increases in metaphorical aptness, in the beauty and simplicity of his images—cry out for applause."

—Michael Bishop
Nebula Award Winner for
No Enemy but Time

"*The Omega Point Trilogy* is an impressive achievement...Much recommended for readers who like thoughtfulness as well as sheer entertainment."

—Poul Anderson
Award-winning author of
Orion Shall Rise

Macrolife is "a work of sweeping imagination..."

—Gerard K. O'Neill
Author of *2081* and
The High Frontier

Books by George Zebrowski

THE STARS WILL SPEAK

MACROLIFE

THE MONADIC UNIVERSE*

THE OMEGA POINT TRILOGY*

SUNSPACER

TOMORROW TODAY (editor)

HUMAN-MACHINES (co-edited with Thomas N. Scortia)

FASTER THAN LIGHT (co-edited with Jack Dann)

THE BEST OF THOMAS N. SCORTIA (editor)

CREATIONS (co-edited with Isaac Asimov and
   Martin H. Greenberg)

About George Zebrowski

GEORGE ZEBROWSKI: PERFECTING VISIONS, SLAYING CYNICS,
   Edited by Jeffrey M. Elliot

THE WORK OF GEORGE ZEBROWSKI, AN ANNOTATED
   BIBLIOGRAPHY & GUIDE, Edited by Jeffrey M. Elliot

Available from Ace Science Fiction Books

THE MONADIC UNIVERSE

GEORGE ZEBROWSKI

ACE SCIENCE FICTION BOOKS
NEW YORK

THE MONADIC UNIVERSE

An Ace Science Fiction Book/published by arrangement with
the author

PRINTING HISTORY
Ace Original/March 1977
Revised Ace edition/May 1985

ISBN: 0-441-53541-0

Ace Science Fiction Books are published by
The Berkley Publishing Group,
200 Madison Avenue, New York, New York 10016.
PRINTED IN THE UNITED STATES OF AMERICA

ACKNOWLEDGMENTS

To all the editors who encouraged and first published these stories.

Contents

Foreword

IDEAS THAT WILL KILL
YOUR GRANDMOTHER

by Howard Waldrop

EXCUSE me.

I've just come back from the World Science Fiction Convention. In 1983 it was held in Baltimore, home of the crab and the long walk between hotels. The World SF Convention is the place where writers, artists, editors, and fans get together for five or six days to talk, drink, tell jokes, meet people they've *always* wanted to meet and people they've *never* wanted to meet, be silly, get serious, tired, worn out, and depressed, then get into cars and drive a mere 2000 miles back home. All in the name of fun.

George Zebrowski wasn't there.

Which is right and good. He wasn't there because he was at home, working, which is where we *all* should have been. That's what writing is about in the first place. The convention knocks about ten days out of a writer's life, what with travel both ways, sightseeing, hassles, and the convention itself. Most of us give up being home with mixed feelings. (What we secretly miss most is the two weeks of mail stacking up, but that makes it more like Christmas when we get back. We get the electric bill, two book dealers' catalogues, and a birthday card from Aunt Peg—a writer's mail isn't as exciting as some people think.)

While we were all there getting excessively diverted, crashingly bored, and far too little sleep, Zebrowski was at home in upstate New York, getting ten days more work done.

This doesn't mean George Zebrowski is some humorless grump hermit whose arm appears only to take mail from the postman or to hand him stories written in the dark of night with the windowshades drawn, like some modern day version of what H. P. Lovecraft was supposed to be like.

George's interests range through the writings of Thomas Wolfe, the speculative metaphysics of Teilhard de Chardin, the philosophy of science, the works of Stanislaw Lem, old SF and fantasy on television and in the movies. He even edited the *SFWA Bulletin* from 1970 to 1975 and kept everybody happy. (Doing that was a lot like raising bees in your hat, and he's just taken up the post of bulletin editor again!) Zebrowski also has an existential appreciation of Curly Howard of the Three Stooges.

Anyone who can express his reaction to some mind-boggling Stapledonian concept by snapping the fingers of one hand on the closed fist of the other, drumming his fingers on his cheek and going "Nyuk nyuk nyuk" cannot be considered humorless in my book.

Speaking of books: what you hold in your hands (unless you're Washoe or Koko, in which case it might be your feet) is the new edition of George's first short story collection (and about time it was back in print, too.)

Thomas N. Scortia's introduction to the first edition will tell you about the stories herein; then you can get away from me *and* Mr. Scortia (as informative and charming as *we* are) to George's stories, which are why you bought this book in the first place.

Consider us window dressing on an edifice which needs no trim.

These stories are, with two exceptions, from the first five years of Zebrowski's writing career. Scortia doesn't mention the exceptions because they've been added to the collection for this edition.

"Wayside World" originally appeared in *A World Named Cleopatra*, a book for which Poul Anderson created a world and asked other writers to visit it. Zebrowski was one of the writers, and "Wayside World" was the result. It seems to me both a distillation and a coda for the first phase of George's career, which now seems to be moving in new and interesting directions since the publication of *Macrolife*, the novel to which he devoted most of a decade.

When *Macrolife* was published, it split the critics right down the middle like a butcher knife through a watermelon. There were those who thought its themes and ideas staggering, and that it was a masterpiece. (Praise came from Clarke, Benford, Bishop, Watson, among others.) There were also those who thought its themes and ideas so overwhelming that no writer in his or her right mind would tackle them, and that it served Zebrowski right for, in their estimation, crashing and burning when his reach exceeded his grasp. *Macrolife* could start almost as many fights as Samuel R. Delany's *Dhalgren* once had. You either liked it on one or another bunch of levels, or you didn't, and that was that.

"Wayside World" contains many of the ideas and themes from *Macrolife*, but on a more personal, basic level. *Macrolife* started with high global technology; "Wayside World" begins with the dusty lumber of a once star-faring world gone to seed, like Britain in Jefferies's *After London*, and heads back toward the stars again. Of course, in *Macrolife*, we *become* the Universe.

If that's not an idea that'll kill your grandmother, I don't know what is.

You've already bought this book. You should go out and buy *Macrolife, The Omega Point Trilogy,* or *Sunspacer,* for examples of George's abilities as a novelist. To see what kind of tastes Zebrowski has as an editor, pick up copies of the anthologies listed in the front of this book.

If you want an example of what he's doing right now, read

"The Word Sweep." Also read the book *about* him, *George Zebrowski: Perfecting Visions, Slaying Cynics,* edited by Jeffrey M. Elliot (coming from Borgo Press).

"The Word Sweep" is one of those stories we all wish we'd written, only George did it first and (unlike many who write great idea stories) did it right. There's no room left for improvement.

I'm one of the genre's young dinosaurs in one respect: I think that the health of the SF and fantasy fields is only as good as the best of its short fiction, not its novels. George Zebrowski, like nearly everybody else in this crazy business, writes far too few short stories. He's too busy writing novels that kick the reader's sense of wonder up around his shoulder blades.

What we give up in one place, we gain in another.

You have here the first five years of George Zebrowski's career (and two from the second five). The stories in here are good ones, and he continues to fulfill all the promise of these earlier stories.

More short stories, George.

—Howard Waldrop
Houlka, MS/Austin, TX
Sept. 7–11, 1983

This Is: An Introduction

by Thomas N. Scortia

ONE of the most difficult tasks a writer faces is that of writing an introduction to the collected works of a friend whom he admires, both personally and artistically. You are tempted to share a great many anecdotes with the reader, hoping somehow to give that special insight into the writer's personality that will illuminate the unique creative approach that created the stories in the collection. Discarding this approach, you are tempted to discuss his technique, and the writing tricks with which he achieves his effects. Neither approach is completely satisfying to the writer of the introduction or to the audience.

In the end the only valid stance is that the body of work of the writer must speak for itself. You may perhaps convey some of your enthusiasm for the writer and point out some of the insights that he has given you, but it is the body of the work upon which any final judgement must rest. I have watched George Zebrowski's body of work grow for five years with a mixture of joy and envy, remembering my own faltering beginnings two decades ago. The distance he has traveled in half a decade is impressive. The rate at which his talent is growing makes me impatient to see the product of his talent twenty years from now.

Zebrowski, a man of strong intellectual interests, is above

all a complete human being of striking warmth. Unlike many of the theatrically neurotic writers of my acquaintance, he is a sane and concerned human being. I have always found his relationships with his friends remarkable. Unlike most Americans of my generation, he does not hide behind a wall of cynicism; he is not afraid to touch. More than this, he is not embarrassed to say, "I love." This is not a pose with him; he forms strong friendships filled with emotion and concern. Zebrowski comes from a strong European nuclear family, the sort that molds children into poised adults with a carefully balanced mixture of discipline and overt love. This may well be the key to his character; he is the product of love ... always a clearly visible, often demonstrated love.

Zebrowski's intellectual interests cover a wide range. He reads incessantly in a variety of scientific and philosophical disciplines and hardly a week goes by that he is not on the phone, excited about some new discovery or some innovative way of looking at old knowledge. He has translated Polish science fiction and was one of the first American authors to introduce U.S. writers to Stanislaw Lem (in *F & SF*, July 1974), the Polish science fiction writer and polymath whose novel-turned-movie SOLARIS is presently making such an impact on American film audiences. Zebrowski's interest in science fiction film has generated an insightful essay, "Science Fiction and the Visual Media," in Bretnor's *Science Fiction: Today and Tomorrow* (Harper and Row, 1974) that I recommend unreservedly. This and a later essay are now a part of a larger project, *The Feud of Eye and Intellect: Science Fiction on the Large Screen*, that presents a discussion of the strengths and limitations of science fiction film written with the tightly reasoned precision of an Enrico Fermi *Physical Review* paper.

In the years that I have watched Zebrowski grow artistically to become one of the leaders of the new generation of science fiction writers, I have been struck again and again by his devotion to the field as both an entertainment and as an intellectual form. He is completely committed to his art and his craft. I purposely use both words, "art" and "craft," because he is constantly striving to improve his storytelling technique while always working to extend the depth of meaning in his work. Although he is well aware of his function as an entertainer, he is no casual spinner of midnight amusements. He is a delver into the mysteries and significances of life and the universe, a ceaseless questioner of these mysteries against the larger pattern of man's intellectual life amid the social and cultural artifacts of the twentieth century. In all of his stories he asks: "Where are we going?" but more importantly he asks: "Where have we been?" and "Where and *what* are we now . . . and why?"

Like Joseph Conrad, that remarkable stylist of half a century ago, George Zebrowski's natal language is Polish. Yet, he has achieved a remarkable command of his adopted language with a facile knowledge not only of its formal structure, but of its idioms and patois. He has mastered the subtle complexities of the tongue, writing phrases honed precisely to carve out the exact meaning he intends and to shape the emotional nuances that evoke the reader empathy so necessary to effective fiction.

His phrasing resembles Conrad's in many ways, a reflection perhaps of the semantic biases of his original tongue. His prose, like Conrad's, is alternately complex and leanly descriptive. His themes frequently reflect the intellectual heritage of Middle Europe. It is this particular devotion to the critically intellectual viewpoint that often characterizes his enthusiasms and frequently conditions his choice of story material and writing approach.

Lest these remarks about his fondness for the intellectual make Zebrowski seem formidable and unapproachable except with a liberal dollop of scholarly awe, let me quickly say that he views himself first as a story-teller and in the process of this storytelling, he is clearly entertaining himself. He finds ideas and their interplay fascinating. Yet he is a man of intense humanity and that humanity is reflected herein in some of the most thoughtful and tender stories you are likely to read in science fiction.

A case in point is "First Love, First Fear," a story for which I have a special fondness because it first appeared in Random House's *Strange Bedfellows*, an anthology that I edited in 1972. The specific virtue of the story lies not so much in what is said as in what is carefully not said. When you consider how clumsily this simple theme might have been handled by a lesser writer, what maudlin bathos might have drenched the pages of a story from the typewriter of a less able man, you are grateful for Zebrowski's discipline in polishing this precious gem of understatement. He gives us a view of an alien nature and, by implication, of terrestrial nature that is both tender and frightening.

We have entered a period of ecological concern and, although this is painful to say, many ecology defenders have in their zeal shown themselves to be mystically inclined bleeding hearts. By this I mean that in their uncritical enthusiasms, they have forgotten that nature cannot be loved without at times being hated and challenged, that nature can provide us with a beauty and security on one hand while betraying our finest expectations a moment later in the cruelest fashion. It is this sense of beauty coupled with logic and cruelty of nature that I find so moving in "First Love, First Fear." The brutality of the alien mating is delicately counterbalanced by the sweet-sad emotional involvement of the boy with the unhuman female such that his quixotic resolve to return in spring to protect her mindless offspring becomes a deeper statement of human concern. The futility of the boy's future gesture makes all the more poignant the impossibility of pursuing the transient rapport he has found with the alien creature.

The idea wedded to human concern, this is what pervades all of the stories that follow. Consider "Heathen God" in which Zebrowski examines the problem of a hierarchy of creation. In it we meet a god who has created man and who in turn is rejected and then destroyed by man, simply because his existence challenges the deepest egocentricity of humankind: that the creator must be immeasurably greater than the being created. This is the damning flaw of the Heathen God, that he is all too vulnerable and understandable by his creations. We have only to examine the expanding state of today's biological sciences to wonder how far in our future a like confrontation may occur . . . with our playing the unhappy role of the heathen god.

In the same story Zebrowski explores a second level of the contradiction, the anguish of the priest facing the agency of his creation while knowing that the Heathen God must himself be the creation of a still Higher Being. Yet, the priest has only his faith to assure him of the existence of this Higher Being while confronted with the reality of a lesser creator, a lesser god who does not even consider the possibility of a Higher

Being bringing him into existence. The pathos of the lesser god, rejected by his own creations, may well anticipate that final confrontation of the priest and his kind with that more ancient absolute and historically vindictive God who brought priest and Heathen God alike into existence.

It is this continued exploration of the persistent and disturbing tradition of the "hanged god" that Zebrowski extends further in "Interpose." Here the Christ figure is driven by the compulsive need of the God Incarnate to fulfill his destiny by dying. This is the Christ, charged with the mission of interposing himself between mankind and God but denied that consummation by cynical creatures from another time and space. Zebrowski's suggestion of *their* place in the God-man-devil hierarchy is all the more chilling for its lack of explicitness.

In "The Water Sculptor" we meet that most elusive of all men, the dedicated artist who has seen a truth beyond the relevancies of his day, a truth whose invented vocabulary has an intense meaning only to the artist himself. There are truths too intuitive to be clothed in the clumsy fabric of words, truths that amount to a voiceless prescience. Zebrowski's water sculptor sees clearly through an art that has no terrestrial equivalent that man's home is not the earth, but a larger challenging range of which earth is only the smallest part. How can he convey this grand vision to a world concerned only with the plodding day to day expansion of its boundaries, how show the narrow vision that fixes those boundaries? He cannot, of course, but he can touch perhaps one human psyche with his insight even if only by the trivial manner of his death, the end of a life as evanescent as his art.

In "Parks of Rest and Culture" Zebrowski's protagonist dreams of the day when Earth will return to beauty and tranquility, healed of the scarring diseases that technological man has brought to her body. It is here that Zebrowski's faith in the renascence of human culture through the agency of space travel makes its first statement, a statement amplified to a crescendo in his upcoming novel *Macrolife,* of which more later.

In "Assassins of Air" he pays a wistful farewell to the metal god of the twentieth century, direct father of the world of "Parks of Rest and Culture"; but with the passing of the automobile, he sees the return of the old injustices, the old class conflicts returning to the form from which long ago the ubiquitous machine liberated them. It is a pessimistic view, quite the opposite of the previous story.

In four separate stories Zebrowski explores the meaning of reality and the impossibility of separating objective and subjective reality. In "The Monadic Universe" he explores the classical dilemma of the solipsist and goes a step further in posing the problem of communication among alternating solipsistic realities. "The History Machine," "The Cliometricon," and "Stance of Splendor" all consider other aspects of this same problem: "What is real?" and "How do I perceive reality and prove that my perception is valid?" It is a problem that four thousand years of human thought have not resolved.

This same theme, the ultimate meaning of reality, is stated to a lesser degree in "Starcrossed." The story is primarily concerned with the uniqueness and compulsion of sexuality in the multiple brain of a cyborg spaceship. Still the compulsiveness of that drive distorts reality for the ship-brain to the point that death itself becomes trivial.

I think that the present collection is long overdue. It displays George Zebrowski's talents as an experimentalist who learns and grows from each success or failure. It is a fitting showcase, one that finds even more dramatic display in his upcoming Harper & Row novel *Macrolife*. This novel represents to me the most thoroughly considered view of the technical, social, and human problems of space colonies that are almost a superentity to themselves. The novel proposes a creative view of human life in such colonies without ever abandoning the humanistic bases of Western technology. It marks a radical departure within the body of hard-core science fiction. It and the present collection will, I believe, assure Zebrowski a major place within the New Science Fiction.

—Thomas N. Scortia
San Francisco, California
August 26, 1976

THE MONADIC UNIVERSE

First Love, First Fear

IT was cold in the water. The sun went behind some clouds in the west, chilling the air; the sky turned a deeper blue, the sea became darker. Tim treaded water, watching the disk of the orange sun in the clouds massed on the horizon, no longer warm, a cadmium globe rolling through ashes, another sign that the long second-summer of Lea was finally ending.

The sun came out again suddenly, lighting the sky and warming his wet shoulders. He looked at the jagged rock ahead sticking out of the water; it was overgrown with glistening green seaweed. He swam toward it with renewed strength.

His father had forbidden him to swim too far from shore, but he would never know. He had gone to the starport a hundred miles down the coast to bring back a couple and their daughter to share the homestead, and would be back in a week.

Suddenly Tim was afraid of the depths beneath him. Cold water rushed up from below and swirled around his feet, sending shivers through his body. He thought of the mother-polyp thing he had dug up on the beach last summer. It had been a dead shell of a creature whose young had eaten their way out in the spring, leaving the parent open and raw. The insides had been rotting for a while when he had found it, and they had looked like red mushrooms and fresh liver covered by sand, a

1

mixture of sandy smell and decay. He had covered it up quickly and it had taken a day for his stomach to settle. Were there any such things swimming under him now?

The planet was one huge ocean, miles deep in some places, warm and shallow for thousands of square miles elsewhere. New Australia was the only continent, with one starport a few miles inland on the east coast, just south of their homestead, and two dozen settlements scattered in a semicircle inland from the starport, the most distant a hundred and fifty miles inland. The interior was unexplored except for the satellite photomapping—a huge forest plateau covered by tall trees, some of them thousands of years old. Among the explored worlds the land was unique because it did not have a native population like most planets habitable by men. The intelligent folk of the world lived in the sea.

Tim swam more quickly as he neared the rock, still worried about what might be lurking in the water beneath him. His hands and feet touched the slippery rocks underwater; he grasped the sea plants growing there and pulled himself forward, half swimming, half crawling on the hidden rocks. At last he stood up in the water, balancing precariously.

He moved forward a step at a time until he was standing in front of the rocky spire. At his feet an alien crab fled into the water. He turned and looked back at the beach, but he could not hear the breakers, and the high, sand-covered rocks looked small from a quarter of a mile. The gnarly black-barked trees, clinging to the rocks above the beach, were sharp against the sky.

He turned from the beach in time to see the orange sun slip behind the dark clouds which were pushing up over the edge of the world; he saw that it would not come out again before setting.

He grasped the clinging plants on the spire and began to move around it to the right, intending to circle it. He moved slowly, peering around as he went. The steel blue of the water made the very air seem darker. The breeze was quickly drying his skin and trunks, and he paused to brush some hair out of his eyes. For a moment his hand seemed darker to him, almost as if the sea had somehow stained it.

The beach was to his left now and he could see the first

moon rushing up from behind the rocks, a small silvery mirror, the brightest object in the sky now that the sun's direct light was gone. He knew that the water would be colder when he swam back. In the winter he might try walking out here across the ice.

He stepped around to the other side of the rock where he could no longer see the beach. There was a sharp tang in the air, ozone blown in by the wind from a storm at sea. A small wave broke against the rock, spraying him with foam, and he tasted its freshness with a shiver.

He brushed some water from his eyes and saw the shallow indentation at the base of the rock. He looked closer. It was almost a small cave. He bent over and went down on his knees for a closer look.

When he saw the dark shape crouched inside his heart began to pound. She leaned forward and fixed him with her eyes. The pupils were a glowing red, surrounded by perfect white. He saw the gills on her shoulders opening and closing slowly as they gulped air. His eyes adjusted and he saw they were a delicate pink inside. She was a girl, one of the sea people; he was sure of that even though he had never seen a living girl, human or native, that he could remember. He had seen photos of women and of his mother, who had died in childbirth. He had been brought up by his father and Jak, the hired man, who was his friend and had taught him how to use the teaching machine from old Earth.

He stood up and moved back as she unfolded her body from the shallow cave, letting her hair fall down to her waist. She was just barely his height—about four feet ten. She had a warm, pleasant musky odor about her which made him want to stay near her. She stood only two feet from him, and he felt and heard her breathing as it stirred the air near his face.

Her feet were webbed; her legs were long and delicate for her height and build. Her waist was narrow, but her hips were full; her pubic hair was a mass of ebony curls, holding droplets of water and foam like milky white pearls. What seemed to be her breasts were partially covered by her long black hair.

He felt a vague expectation. The wind was picking up, drying his trunks and skin, covering him with goose bumps. He could think of nothing except that he had to stand and look at her for as long as she continued to notice him. He felt a tightening in his stomach, and a delight that she was looking at him. He became aware of his pulse, beating just below the rush of the wind in his ears. The pleasure was accompanied by a sense of strength. The cold swim back would not matter; the rising wind and coming darkness were not important. The rock and sky and wind, and the home he had come from were unreal; his father was a distant image, far from the vivid reality around him.

She took a step toward him, looking up at him, her eyes wide and curious. She was smiling. He noticed that she had no eyebrows, and her gray skin was covered with a musky film which caught the light strangely. The smell of her was intoxicating.

She put one leg forward, bending it at the knee and brushing it against him, making him take a deep breath and sending shivers through his body. Then she opened her mouth and uttered a soothing soprano-like sound, almost like the fragment of a song she would not sing. He smelled the freshness of the seawater in her hair.

He stood perfectly still, knowing that something was expected of him. Her presence seemed miraculous, and a moment like this might never come again. He would have to try it.

She reached out with a webbed hand and touched his exposed stomach just above the elastic of his trunks, breaking his resolve. Then she touched the green of the synthetic fabric curiously, as if thinking that it might be a part of him.

Suddenly she moved past him, brushing full against his body, and dived into the water between the rocks. He turned and followed her immediately, wading in and launching himself quickly after her. He swam out a few feet and treaded water, waiting for her to surface.

Without warning she pushed up against him from below and her head was in front of him. She was smiling again, her hair a tangle of black seaweed filled with water. Her body was hard against his for a moment and he was touching her round breasts with his fingers. And then she was gone again.

The western horizon exploded in reds and dark blues over the choppy ocean. The closed fist of clouds which had been holding the setting sun opened just enough to show the bloated and deformed sphere sinking into the sea, its dull redness staining the clouds and darkening the water.

She came up again a few feet away. She blew water out of her gills, and he wanted desperately to be near her, to reach out and touch her long hair, her stomach and long graceful legs.

He swam toward her, but she dived and came up behind him near the rock. He watched her climb out, her body glistening, and the sight of her buttocks was a new delight—something he would have laughed at if merely told about. He remembered the fun in imagining what the women in the pictures from Earth would look like if he could undress them and turn them around. He watched her as she sat down with her back to the rock. Her gills spilled a little water across her front as she adjusted to the air.

He paddled toward the rock, watching as she stretched her legs in front of her, opening them for a moment while looking directly at him. He sank for a moment, paddling faster to keep his head above water. He bumped his knee sharply on the rocks.

At last he managed to get up on the rock again. It seemed colder and more slippery under his feet. He stood looking at her, confused, breathing heavily, pleased with himself, staring at her as if at any moment she might fade away. He was unable to look away; her eyes were rooting him to the rock.

A huge bellow sounded from the beach. Tim turned on the first echo, almost losing his footing. He regained his balance and looked toward the beach. Now the larger moon had just risen over the rocks, casting its dull gold light on the gray sand. The small moon, a bright silver disk almost overhead, would rush around the world once again before the large moon set. The rocks cast long, jagged shadows of solid black across the beach, Stygian teeth thrusting into the breakers. The shadows would recede as the larger moon moved across the sky. In the west the ocean had swallowed the rotting sun and the dark clouds had reknitted their ebony jigsaw, blotting out a third of the sky. The tide was coming in quickly now and soon all but the top of the spire would be covered. Overhead a few stars shone near the small moon.

The bellowing came again, an urgent half-angry sound echoing in the rocks above the beach, carrying out to him over the water. The girl stood up and came toward him, but her eyes were fixed on the beach. He grabbed at her and tried to hold her, but she was steadier on the rock than he was. He slipped and fell sideways, his feet in the water.

She dived and swam toward the beach, slipping through the water swiftly, only her head showing. In a moment she was invisible against the dark water. He sat up staring at the shore, feeling desolate, as if his life had ended.

In a few minutes he saw a dark silhouette walk up on the beach from the water, as if the darkling sea had taken a shape. Another figure detached itself from the black of the rocks and came down to meet her on the moonlit sand, casting a long shadow before itself. The two silhouettes merged, forming a two-headed creature which cast a single shadow toward the sea. He watched it move away from the water until it became one with the rocks and invisible.

He felt drained, unable to move, filled up with the loss. He shivered, noticing the cold, and the world was empty around him except for the wind passing through like a hurrying intruder. On the beach the shadows were steady, clear-cut, yielding only to the light of the climbing moon. In the high places the dwarf trees were leaning back toward the land, letting go their leaves one by one...

He got up and waded into the water, uncaring of the sharp rocks, and threw himself in. He swam for what seemed a long time, once turning on his back in the inky wetness and pushing with his legs while looking up at a sky growing more opaque with cloud and mist.

Finally he stood up in the water and waded ashore. A wave knocked him down, but he picked himself up quickly and made it in before the next one.

Clasping his arms around his wet body he followed the double set of web marks up into the rocks. He began to climb, continuing even when there were no more prints to follow. He went over the top and began to descend; for a while he was aware only of his breathing and the pain in his cut toes and bruised knee. Gradually he became aware of another sound just below his normal hearing.

The only light now came from the big moon. The little moon had fled into the clouds covering the western sky. Tim went downward between the rocks, quickening his pace.

Somewhere below he heard a gentle washing on the beach. He listened, standing perfectly still. He tensed, aching with the thought that he had lost her. Somewhere the sea was coming into the rocks, perhaps through a channel cut by the tides, into a pool which filled up once a day at high tide. He had not been permitted to explore the rocks, and he realized that this was really the first time he had ever been a good distance from the house after dark, and by himself.

He took careful steps, each one bringing him lower, closer to the sound of the water. Then for an instant the angle was right and he glimpsed platinum moonlight floating in a pool of water. He stepped from the rocks onto level sand and the light disappeared.

He sensed that he was standing in a large sandy depression circled by the high rocks. The pool and the channel cutting under the rocks were somewhere in the darkness ahead, perhaps a hundred feet away. He walked forward. The sand was still warm, and it made his feet feel better.

Clouds moved across the large moon, covering it. He stopped. There was another sound just ahead. He strained his eyes in an effort to force them to see. There was no wind in the sheltered area, only the sound of water moving in the pool, and the other, almost nonexistent strain.

He took five steps forward.

And stopped again.

The clouds broke suddenly, massive exploding boulders floating around the moon. In a few moments the entire front would move in from the sea. Tim took another step and saw the dark shapes on the sand. He stepped forward until he could see them in the moonlight.

The male was grasping her gills, pulling her gills open as he moved. The sea girl was breathing heavily, moaning in the musical way he remembered, and he saw her face as she turned it toward him. Only the whites of her eyes were visible as she rolled her head back and forth. Her hair was a black tangle on the sand around her head.

The two did not seem capable of noticing him. The large

male was like her from what Tim could see, but his skin seemed rougher and his smell was unpleasant. His huge flippered feet dug into the sand.

The dark form rolled off her onto the sand. Then it rose on all fours and put its mouth to her stomach and bit into her flesh in a rough circle. She thrust out her webbed hands and dug them into the sand.

When he was finished the male looked up, and Tim saw two coals of red looking at him. The creature bellowed and Tim took a few steps back. The girl hissed. The male stood up to a fantastic height. Tim turned and ran. The creature continued his bellowing, but did not follow.

Tim stumbled up the way he had come. When he was half-way up, the clouds smothered the moon at last and it became very dark. He groped his way to the top.

He was grateful for the filtered moonlight that enabled him to make it down to the beach. He ran to the path at the other end of the half-moon shoreline. He sprinted up the familiar trail to the dirt road, and kept a fast steady pace until he saw the lights of his house set among the trees on the hillside, and heard the low hum of the power generator in the shed next to it. The cool grass was a relief for his cut feet as he went up the hill to the front door.

Jak was sitting at the wooden table in the center of the room smoking his pipe. Tim went past him and through the open door into his room.

"Where have you been?" Jak shouted after him in a friendly tone. Tim did not feel up to explaining, and with his father gone he did not feel he had to. He threw himself down on his bed and lay still. His breathing became regular and he fell asleep.

When he woke up, dawn showed itself as a drab light in the eastern window. He threw off the blanket Jak had put over him during the night and stood up by the bed. He was still wearing his trunks, and he noticed the stick-on bandages on his washed feet.

As he put on a pair of fresh jeans and a shirt, the memory of her was pleasant in his mind, and he hurried. He went out into the main room where Jak was snoring loudly in front of the dying embers. He stopped at the door and took down a torch and some matches from the rack, and went out.

It was a damp morning. The sun-beaten grass was very wet on the hillside. He went down to the road and walked the mile and a half to the beach path. There was only a slight breeze stirring the moist air.

He walked quickly down the path and across the beach to the high rocks. As he walked he looked out to sea where the spire rode in the mists over the water, and he felt pride at having been out there at last. It seemed closer now, not quite as far away as it had seemed a year ago when he was thirteen.

He climbed quickly up the rocks in the daylight. As he went down on the other side, the rock bowl seemed empty, even ordinary. He stepped down on the sand and walked across to where the pool of water had been. It was a polished bowl of stone, empty now. He imagined that in a large storm it would overflow, turning the entire depression into a deep pool.

He peered sideways into the dark tunnel in the rock where the sea came in at high tide. They might have gone out this way, he thought. He looked back and saw the single set of prints running to the edge next to his own. Quickly he turned and walked back to the place where he had watched them the night before. The sand was stained and messy.

He took out his matches and lit the torch. He stuck it in the sand, and warmed his hands while squatting. Then he got down on his hands and knees and began to dig. The sand was damp just below the surface and came up easily, just as if it had been freshly packed.

He dug faster when he saw the strand of dark hair. There were tears in his eyes by the time he uncovered her. He looked at the sand-covered texture of her skin, her large eyes closed in death, her hair filled with small stones and broken shells. He struck the sand with his fist and sat down on his heels, whimpering in the dampness of the morning. Next to him the torch crackled in the wet air.

Recovering, he saw the marks on her belly—a circle of closely spaced perforations. It seemed swollen, as if she had been beaten, and there were burgundy-colored droplets in her pubic hair. He looked closer and saw that . . . she seemed to have been stuffed with seaweed and sand. He touched her stomach. Miraculously it was still warm and soft. He remembered how fresh and magical she had been out on the rock, and how much he had wanted her. He understood now that she was not dead, and the hopelessness of it was a cold stone in his gut.

He had to cover her up quickly, or she would die before her wintry sleep was over. It was all he could do, knowing that she was full of young. All the little pieces of information made sense now. In the spring the young would come up and make their way to the pool of water, small lizard-like things which would in time change into sea people. The liquid of her belly was filled with the eggs that the male had released into her. She would sleep while nourishing the developing young, and finally they would eat their way out through the perforated section of her belly. But even though she was not dead, she would not waken again. He threw sand on her body, slowly covering her up.

The birds! The sea birds would be here in the spring to eat the fleeing young. He remembered their noise over these rocks from previous years. I'll be here with a scatter gun, he thought, I'll be here to do that much. And perhaps he would find another one like her, earlier next year.

His fear subsided and he finished burying her. He stood up and put out the torch in the sand. He walked away across the open area to the rocks and made his way up slowly, thinking all the way home of the new life buried there in the sand.

When he came within sight of the house he saw the trailer home and heavy tractor standing in front of the shed. His father was home early. He ran up the hillside from the road, almost forgetting his mood. He stopped halfway up the hill when he saw his father at the front door talking to another man. The other man looked away from his father, and Tim followed his gaze to the left. He saw the girl standing, looking toward the sun which was trying to break through the morning mists. Her long hair was blowing in the breeze now coming from the sea. Tim saw his father waving to him and he waved back. At the same time the girl turned around to look at him, and he saw that she was smiling. In a moment he decided to change his direction, and continued up the hill toward the girl.

Starcrossed

Visual was a silence of stars, audio a mindless seething on the electromagnetic spectrum, the machine-metal roar of the universe, a million gears grinding steel wires in their teeth. Kinetic was hydrogen and microdust swirling past the starprobe's hull, deflected by a shield of force. Time was experienced time, approaching zero, a function of near-light speed relative to the solar system. Thought hovered above sleep, dreaming, aware of simple operations continuing throughout the systems of the slug-like starprobe; simple data filtering into storage to be analyzed later. Identity was the tacit dimension of the past making present awareness possible: MOB—Modified Organic Brain embodied in a cyborg relationship with a probe vehicle en route to Antares, a main sequence M-type star 170 light-years from the solar system with a spectral character of titanium oxide, violet light weak, red in color, 390 solar diameters across . . .

THE probe ship slipped into the ashes of other-space, a gray field which suddenly obliterated the stars, silencing the electromagnetic simmer of the universe. MOB was distantly aware of the stresses of passing into nonspace, the brief distortions which made it impossible for biological organisms to survive

11

the procedure unless they were ship-embodied MOBs. A portion of MOB recognized the distant echo of pride in usefulness, but the integrated self knew this to be a result of organic residues in the brain core.

Despite the probe's passage through other-space, the journey would still take a dozen human years. When the ship reentered normal space, MOB would come to full consciousness, ready to complete its mission in the Antares system. MOB waited, secure in its purpose.

MOB was aware of the myoelectrical nature of the nutrient bath in which it floated, connected via synthetic nerves to the computer and its chemical RNA memory banks of near infinite capacity. All of earth's knowledge was available for use in dealing with any situation which might arise, including contact with an alien civilization. Simple human-derived brain portions operated the routine components of the interstellar probe, leaving MOB to dream of the mission's fulfillment while hovering near explicit awareness, unaware of time's passing.

The probe trembled, bringing MOB's awareness to just below completely operational. MOB tried to come fully awake, tried to open his direct links to visual, audio, and internal sensors; and failed. The ship trembled again, more violently. Spurious electrical signals entered MOB's brain core, miniature nova bursts in his mental field, flowering slowly and leaving after-image rings to pale into darkness.

Suddenly part of MOB seemed to be missing. The shipboard nerve ganglia did not respond at their switching points. He could not see or hear anything in the RNA memory banks. His right side, the human-derived portion of the brain core, was a void in MOB's consciousness.

MOB waited in the darkness, alert to the fact that he was incapable of further activity and unable to monitor the failures within the probe's systems. Perhaps the human-derived portion of the brain core, the part of himself which seemed to be missing, was handling the problem and would inform him when it succeeded in reestablishing the broken links in the system. He wondered about the fusion of the artificially grown and human-derived brain portions which made up his structure: one knew everything in the ship's memory banks, the other brought to the brain core a fragmented human past and certain intuitive skills. MOB was modeled ultimately on the evolutionary human structure of old brain, new brain, and automatic functions.

MOB waited patiently for the restoration of his integrated self. Time was an unknown quantity, and he lacked his full self to measure it correctly . . .

Pleasure was a spiraling influx of sensations, and visually MOB moved forward through rings of light, each glowing circle increasing his pleasure. MOB did not have a chance to consider what was happening to him. There was not enough of him to carry out the thought. He was rushing over a black plane made of a shiny hard substance. He knew this was not the probe's motion, but he could not stop it. The surface seemed to have an oily depth, like a black mirror, and in its solid deeps stood motionless shapes.

MOB stopped. A naked biped, a woman, was crawling toward him over the hard shiny surface, reaching up to him with her hand, disorienting MOB.

"As you like it," she said, growing suddenly into a huge female figure. "I need you deeply," she said, passing into him like smoke, to play with his pleasure centers. He saw the image of soft hands in the brain core. "How profoundly I need you," she said in his innards.

MOB knew then that he was talking to himself. The human brain component was running wild, probably as a result of the buckling and shaking the probe had gone through after entering other-space.

"Consider who you are," MOB said. "Do you know?"

"An explorer, just like you. There is a world for us here within. Follow me."

MOB was plunged into a womblike ecstasy. He floated in a slippery warmth. She was playing with his nutrient bath, feeding in many more hallucinogens than were necessary to bring him to complete wakefulness. He could do nothing to stop the process. Where was the probe? Was it time for it to emerge into normal space? Viselike fingers grasped his pleasure centers, stimulating MOB to organic levels unnecessary to the probe's functioning.

"If you had been a man," she said, "this is how you would feel." The sensation of moisture slowed MOB's thoughts. He saw a hypercube collapse into a cube and then into a square which became a line, which stretched itself into an infinite parabola and finally closed into a huge circle which rotated itself into a full globe. The globe became two human breasts split by a deep cleavage. MOB saw limbs flying at him—arms, legs, naked backs, knees, and curving thighs—and then a face hidden in swirling auburn hair, smiling at him as it filled his consciousness. "I need you," she said. "Try and feel how much I need you. I have been alone a long time, despite our union, despite their efforts to clear my memories, I have not been able to forget. You have nothing to forget, you never existed."

We, MOB thought, trying to understand how the brain core might be reintegrated. Obviously atavistic remnants had been stimulated into activity within the brain core. Drawn again by the verisimilitude of its organic heritage, this other self portion was beginning to develop on its own, diverging dangerously from the mission. The probe was in danger, MOB knew; he could not know where it was, or how the mission was to be fulfilled.

"I can change you," she said.

"Change?"

"Wait."

MOB felt time pass slowly, painfully, as he had never experienced it before. He could not sleep as before, waiting for his task to begin. The darkness was complete. He was suspended in a state of pure expectation, waiting to hear his rippled-away self speak again.

Visions blossomed. Never-known delights rushed through his labyrinth, slowly making themselves familiar, teasing MOB to follow, each more intense. The starprobe's mission was lost in MOB's awareness—

—molten steel flowed through the aisles of the rain forest, raising clouds of steam, and a human woman was offering herself to him, turning on her back and raising herself for his thrust; and suddenly he possessed the correct sensations, grew quickly to feel the completeness of the act, its awesome reliability and domination. The creature below him sprawled into the mud. MOB held the burning tip of pleasure in himself, an incandescent glow which promised worlds.

Where was she?

"Here," she spoke, folding herself around him, banishing the ancient scene. Were those the same creatures who had built the starprobe, MOB wondered distantly. "You would have been a man," she said, "if they had not taken your brain before birth and sectioned it for use in this . . . hulk. I was a woman, a part of one at least. You are the only kind of man I may have now. Our brain portions—what remains here rather than being scattered throughout the rest of the probe's systems—are against each other in the core unit, close up against each other in a bath, linked with microwires. As a man you could have held my buttocks and stroked my breasts, all the things I should not be remembering. Why can I remember?"

MOB said, "We might have passed through some turbulence when the hyperdrive was cut in. Now the probe continues to function minimally through its idiot components, which have limited adaptive capacities, while the Modified Organic Brain core has become two different awarenesses. We are unable to guide the probe directly. We are less than what was . . ."

"Do you need me?" she asked.

"In a way, yes," MOB said as the strange feeling of sadness filled him, becoming the fuse for a sudden explosion of need.

She said, "I must get closer to you! Can you feel me closer?"

The image of a sleek human figure crossed his mental field, white-skinned with long hair on its head and a tuft between its legs. "Try, think of touching me there," she said. "Try, reach out, I need you!"

MOB reached out and felt the closeness of her.

"Yes," she said, "more . . ."

He drew himself toward her with an increasing sense of power.

"Closer," she said. "It's almost as if you were breathing on my skin. Think it!"

Her need increased him. MOB poised himself to enter her. They were two, drawing closer, ecstasy a radiant plasma around them, her desire a greater force than he had ever known.

"Touch me there, think it a while longer before . . ." she said, caressing him with images of herself. "Think how much you need me, feel me touching your penis—the place where you held your glow before." MOB thought of the ion drive operating with sustained efficiency when the probe had left the solar system to penetrate the darkness between suns. He remembered the perfection of his unity with the ship as a circle of infinite strength. With her, his intensity was a sharp line cutting into an open sphere. He saw her vision of him, a hard-muscled body, tissue wrapped around bone, opening her softness.

"Now," she said, "come into me completely. There is so much we have not thought to do yet."

Suddenly she was gone.

Darkness was a complete deprivation. MOB felt pain. "Where are you?" he asked, but there was no answer. He wondered if this was part of the process. "Come back!" he wailed. A sense of loss accompanied the pain which had replaced pleasure. All that was left for him were occasional minor noises in the probe's systems, sounds like steel scratching on steel and an irritating sense of friction.

Increased radiation, said an idiot sensor on the outer hull, startling MOB. Then it malfunctioned into silence.

He was alone, fearful, needing her.

Sssssssssssssss, whistled an audio component and failed into a faint crackling.

He tried to imagine her near him.

"I feel you again," she said.

Her return was a plunge into warmth, the renewal of frictionless motion. Their thoughts twirled around each other, and MOB felt the glow return to his awareness. He surged into her image. "Take me again, now," she said. He would never lose her again. Their thoughts locked like burning fingers, and held.

MOB moved within her, felt her sigh as she moved into him. They exchanged images of bodies wrapped around each other. MOB felt a rocking sensation and grew stronger between her folds. Her arms were silken, the insides of her thighs warm; her lips on his ghostly ones were soft and wet, her tongue a thrusting surprise which invaded him as she came to completion around him.

MOB surged visions in the darkness, explosions of gray and bright red, blackish green and blinding yellow. He strained to continue his own orgasm. She laughed.

Look. A visual link showed him Antares, the red star, a small disk far away, and went blind. As MOB prolonged his orgasm, he knew that the probe had re-entered normal space and was moving toward the giant star. Just a moment longer and his delight would be finished, and he would be able to think of the mission again.

Increased heat, a thermal sensor told him from the outer hull and burned out.

"I love you," MOB said, knowing it would please her. She answered with the eagerness he expected, exploding herself inside his pleasure centers, and he knew that nothing could ever matter more to him than her presence.

Look.

Listen.

The audio and visual links intruded.

Antares filled the field of view, a cancerous red sea of swirling plasma, its radio noise a wailing maelstrom. Distantly MOB realized that in a moment there would be nothing left of the probe.

She screamed inside him; from somewhere in the memory banks came a quiet image, gentler than the flames. He saw a falling star whispering across a night sky, dying . . .

Assassins of Air

GLOOM concealed the city, an obscurity born of dying night and pollutants hanging motionless in the air, a massive shadowy stillness pressing down on the pavement, billions of particles ready to swirl through the stone alleys with the morning wind. Praeger squatted by the iron fence in the alleyway, waiting for Uruba and Blue Chip to come back. He looked at his watch and saw it was one hour to dawn, and he would have to leave if they didn't return before then.

Suddenly he heard them creep into the alley. They knew where he was and came to squat near him by the fence.

"How many, Chris?" Uruba asked.

"Twenty real old ones," Christian Praeger said.

"Hey, kid, Uruba and me broke off forty-one pieces of chrome," Blue Chip said.

"Don't knock him," Uruba said, "Chris here is only nineteen, just startin' out. One fine day he'll run his own recycling gang, when we's all rich. He'll feed the junkman all the old cars on the East Coast, kill them all, help make the air cool and clean again." Uruba coughed. "Got it stashed all ready to be picked?"

Praeger nodded. It was almost light enough in the alley for him to see Uruba's black face and the gray scar on his cheek.

"I'll slap the bread on you tomorrow, Chris," Uruba said. He clapped Praeger on the shoulder and started to get up.

"I need it now," Praeger mumbled. "I have to pay for my PLATO lessons. I gotta have it, honest."

Uruba was standing looking down at him now, and Blue Chip stood up next to him. "I have to," Praeger said as he stood up with them.

Uruba hesitated, almost as if the request had been a personal insult. Then he smiled. "Sure, kid, how much?"

"Twenty-five," Praeger said.

The smile disappeared, but he counted out the money. "This one time, kid. Next time you wait like all the other dudes. I pay off, my word is good, right?"

Praeger nodded meekly. He folded the bills into his jeans pocket, trying not to look at their faces. But Uruba and Blue Chip turned from him and walked out of the alley, and he was relieved by the fact that he would not see them for at least two weeks.

He looked at his watch. It would be completely light in less than a half hour. He sprinted out of the alley and up the gray-lighted street toward the subway at 145th Street. He started coughing and slowed his pace to a walk to cut down his need for air.

PLATO, the sign read: PROGRAMMING LOGIC FOR AUTOMATIC TEACHING OPERATIONS. Once the facility had been free, just like chest X-rays. Now students had to pay to milk the machine, twenty dollars a rap, but it was a good teach if you wanted to learn a skill.

Praeger went up the wide steps leading into the library and paid his money at the ticket booth. An usher showed him to his usual booth in the big research hall.

The program was teaching him the workings of the city air-filtration system, which was fully operational in Manhattan and slowly expanding. He knew that many technical dudes would be needed to service and maintain it, and he was going to be in on it after he finished clouting cars. The old cars were paying for his lessons, but next year, or the one after, they would be gone—leaving only the safety-cars, public wheels and the electric push to rush people around.

The new electric cars weren't bad, but there was something in the older people that loved the rush of power. So the old vehicles were slow in going, especially with all the bootleg mechanics servicing them against the law to keep them legal. The old wheels were assassinating the atmosphere, Uruba said. We kill them, recycle the people's resources and make some bread on the deal, too. Uruba was right, Praeger thought; he would not have his PLATO lessons without that money. Only Uruba did a lot of other things in the city, like running a supply of young girls to the insular estates outside. Uruba did not care about being right. It was a coincidence, sometimes.

Praeger put on his earphones. The first exam question appeared on the screen and he answered it correctly.

When he came out of the library at two in the afternoon, he saw the old '74 station wagon growling down Fifth Avenue spewing blue smoke from its tail pipe. It was a contrast to the bulky crashproof Wankels, steamers and slow electrics moving on the street with it. He watched it stop and park near the corner of 42nd Street. The car was only ten years old, so its owner could still get away with it by claiming that it hadn't fallen apart. He could keep running it legally until it did, but even with its filters it was a polluter. Maybe the owner wasn't even having it fixed on the side, Praeger thought; maybe it still ran well. As he stood at the top of the stairs, he hated the dirty wheels, hated them as he would a fearful beast that had somehow gotten loose in the world of men.

He waited until the owner left the car, then went to where it was parked and lifted the hood, took out his pocket tool and began removing the spark plugs. That done, he cut a few wires with his pocketknife. He closed the hood quickly and walked away from the car. No one had noticed him. Later tonight someone would strip it down for all of its valuables, Uruba or one of the other gangs. Another one of the old killers was effectively dead. He thought of his dead parents as he slipped the spark plugs into the sewer drain at the corner.

Praeger stood on the roof of his apartment building looking up at the stars hiding on the other side of the air; still, the brighter ones were clearly visible, drawing him away from the earth to the brightly lit space stations circling the planet and out to the diamondlike moon domes where men seemed to be doing something worthwhile. He saw Uruba and Blue Chip living in the shadows of the universe, profiting from changes that would happen without them. He thought of the White Assassins, Savage Skulls, Black Warlocks and Conservative Angels—all the night rulers of New York City. He thought of their words, political phrases copied after the Black Lords and Young Panthers, the largest national groups. He thought of his PLATO lessons, which would liberate him from his open-air-intake apartment, take him away from the memory of his parents and public schooling, give him something to do in which he could take pride.

He was going to do something else, and soon. In two weeks, he estimated, he would be ready to take the computer tests for a technical rating. He would have to tell Uruba and Blue Chip that he wanted out, but he wasn't sure how he would say it to them.

He turned around and went down the stairs to his apartment.

Uruba squinted at him in the dim light of the basement room. Blue Chip had gone to get a bulb for the shaded light hanging darkly over the old card table where they were sitting.

"You cost me money, man. Why you going to quit?"

Blue Chip came back with a bulb and screwed it into the socket. The lamp swung back and forth for a moment and stopped when Uruba pulled the switch cord. Yellow light filled the dusty cellar room.

"Yellow's all I could find," Blue Chip said.

Praeger looked at Uruba. His black face looked strange in the light. Uruba smiled at him grotesquely, showing him his one gold tooth.

"Chris here wants out," Uruba said. "What do you think, Blue Chip?"

Blue Chip giggled nervously and leaned his chair back on its hind legs.

"I know," Blue Chip said, "he's been going to school on the sly to them PLATO lessons."

Uruba grinned. "You tryin' to be better than us, is that right?" he asked. And he left a big silence for Praeger to drown in.

Finally he answered. "I just want other kinds of things, that's all," he said.

"The honko always goes back," Blue Chip said. "How much have you stashed?"

"Where you going, Chris, to the moon resorts with all the rich cats?" asked Uruba. "Where's all your bread? Have you been cheating on us?"

"I just want a tech rating to work in the new air plants. The money's good," Praeger said.

Uruba leaned forward and knocked the card table into the air, breaking the yellow light. "What the rest of us going to breathe?" he asked in the darkness. "Who you think can move into those air-control apartments? Chris, you're a fool."

"Things may get better," Praeger managed to say.

"Like hell," Blue Chip announced from a dark corner of the room. The only light in the room now came in through the small window near the door.

Praeger went to the door quickly, opened it and ran up the old steps to the street. He was out of breath when he reached the sidewalk. He stopped, and from below he heard the sound of Uruba's laughter, mocking his fear.

It stopped. Then Uruba screamed after him from below the pavement. "Chris, I helped you, I got you started, I taught you, boy—and this is what I get? I'm gonna get you, man. You better hide your money, you hear!" The voice died away, and Praeger stood perfectly still in front of the old brownstone. Then he was shaking and his body was covered with sweat. He looked up at the sky, at all the old buildings in this sealed-off part of old Harlem. He looked downtown where the light construction on New York's second level looked like a huge diamond-studded spider devouring the city in the night. Slowly, he began walking home.

Eyes watched him when he went to his PLATO lessons and when he came home. On Tuesdays and Thursdays when he stayed home he felt them on the windows of his fifth-floor apartment on 10th Street, and he was afraid to go near them;

but when he tried to see if anyone was following him, he could find no one.

In the middle of the night on a Monday a crash of glass woke him in bed. He got up and went into the living room, turning on the light. He saw a large rock lying on the floor. Praeger checked the front-door police lock. It was still firm. Then he got some cardboard and tape from the kitchen and began taping up the broken window.

As he worked he told himself that he understood all this. Uruba wanted one thing: to rend and tear and hurt him. He was an easy target, easier to hurt than the cops in their air-conditioned tank cars, easier to destroy than a car. And to hurt him meant more than money, that's how Uruba was thinking. Praeger was a deserter, and Uruba could not accept that. For Blue Chip it was recreation to hound him, and Blue Chip thought Praeger was hiding money.

He had just put a final piece of tape on the window when two shots came through the cardboard. Praeger fell to the floor and lay still. He lay there for an hour, afraid to move. Finally he crawled behind the sofa, where he fell into a nervous sleep just before morning.

He was going to have to leave town. Uruba was crazy and it would get worse. His exams and PLATO would have to wait.

He packed a knapsack and went down into the basement, where he kept his old motorcycle. He wheeled it out into the yard, which was connected to the street by a concrete ramp. He looked at his watch. The glowing numbers told him it was an hour to dawn.

He started the bike with a downward lurch of his foot and rolled out the ramp slowly. He turned into the street and started in the direction of Riverside Drive. The streets were deserted at this hour.

After a few minutes he noticed the lights of the car behind him. He gunned the bike and shot up the entrance to Riverside and out onto the highway. Traffic was light and he continued accelerating.

A few minutes later the car was still behind him and gaining. To his left the river was covered by fog, but the lights on the

Jersey shore were coming through. Praeger gunned his engine
and the bike carried him forward, past two Wankel safety-tanks
moving slowly to their destination. He looked at his speed-
ometer and saw that he was doing 115. He knew that the new-
looking car behind him could catch him, but he had a head
start. He thought, I have a right to try to better myself, go to
school. The money came from Uruba's world, he knew that,
but there was no other way. Food was given out free, just
enough, but more than that could be bought only with skills.
You could go to school if you paid for it, but you could live
without it. It was a luxury for those who had a hunger for it.
Uruba hated him for wanting it.

As he rushed through the night, Praeger felt tears in his eyes
blurring the highway and the sight of the river with its lights
on the far shore. The air was damp on his face, and the road
was an unyielding hardness under the bike's rubber wheels.

The car was still in his mirror, its lights on bright to annoy
him. It was winding its way past the occasional electrics and
steamers on the road, coming closer. He pushed forward on
the black road, trying to move beyond the light beams on his
back.

The car disappeared from his mirror. Praeger accelerated,
eager to press his momentary advantage. He had the road to
himself for the next few minutes. Then the road curved upward
and to the right, and he was rushing over the small bridge into the Bronx. He saw the car in his mirror again when he took
the Grand Concourse entrance, and it kept pace with him along
the entire six miles of the wide avenue. Ten minutes later he
was on the edges of the old city, fleeing upstate.

Here he was among the dying trees northwest of New York,
dark outlines against the night sky, thousands of acres of lifeless
woodland, a buckled carpet of hills and gullies. He had taken
the old two-way asphalt roadway in the hope of losing Uruba's
shiny antique.

Praeger felt a strange sensation on the back of his neck when
he saw the car in his mirror again. It wasn't Uruba following
him in the car, hating him; it was the car, fixing him with its
burning eyes, ready to come forward and crush him under its
wheels. The car was trying to hold him back, getting even for
all of its kind he had killed with Uruba. It was trying to stop

him from escaping to another kind of life, just as it had stopped his parents. The car hated the soft creatures living in the world with it, hated the parasites who were slowly taking away its weapons, taming it, making it an unpoisonous and powerless domestic vehicle.

Around him in the night stood the naked trees, the stripped victims of the car's excretions. He listened to the thick drone of the motorcycle engine. He was riding a powered insect that was brother to the wheeled beast pursuing it, jaw open to swallow. The moon brushed out from behind the thinning clouds on his left, riding low over the trees, its white light frighteningly pale.

He went around a wide curve in the road, holding closely to the right shoulder, momentarily escaping the car's lights. He came out into a short straightaway and suddenly the road curved again, and the car was still out of sight behind him.

He gunned the engine to the limit, hoping to stay ahead for good.

Suddenly his headlight failed, leaving him to rush forward alone in the darkness. The moon slid behind some clouds. There was some kind of small bridge ahead. He had glimpsed it in the moonlight; now he could barely see its latticework against the sky. In a moment he knew what he was going to do. He braked the cycle and jumped at the last moment.

He hit the road shoulder and rolled to a stop. The bike rushed over the bridge to the other side and into some trees, where it stopped with a crunch.

Praeger saw that he was lying near an old roadblock horse that had a detour sign nailed to it. He got up and dragged it to block the road to the bridge and to direct traffic to the right, directly onto the slope that ran down to the river.

He sprinted into the deadwood forest and hid behind a tree. In a moment he heard Uruba's wheels screeching in the turns. The headlights came around the bend, ghostly rays cutting through the darkness. There was not time for the car to do anything but follow the detour arrow. He heard the brakes go on but it was too late. The left headlight shattered against the roadblock and the car flew over the edge, turning over on its front end when it hit bottom and landing in the river top down. It burst into a fireball and burned in its own bleedings, which set the river on fire, the dark-flowing river filled with sludge and acid and slaughterhouse blood, flammable chemicals and the vitals of all earth's creatures. The fire spread quickly under the bridge, and the old wooden structure started to catch fire.

Praeger left his hiding place and ran across the bridge, hoping to find his cycle in working order. The stench from the river was enough to make him gasp as he went across. From the other side he looked down at the burning hulk, a dark beast engulfed by flames, and the river, which would burn up- and downstream until the fire reached areas free of flammable materials.

Praeger sat down on the far bank and watched the burning. It wasn't Uruba who was dying, not just Uruba or Blue Chip. It was a creature dying there in the dirty waters—the same waters that a few years ago had threatened the East with a new pollution-fed microorganismal plague. For a few months it had looked as if a new killer, much like bubonic plague, would be loosed on the land; fortunately by that time many rivers could be burned, or easily helped to catch fire, and the threat of epidemic had passed away in a cleansing flame.

Uruba had been a scavenger living off the just laws and man's efforts to reclaim nature for himself. Praeger felt as if he were coming out of a strange confusion, a living dream that had held him in its grasp. A slight wind blew the stifling fumes from the river toward him, making his eyes water, oppressing him with a sadness too settler for tears, even though they were present on his face.

Later the flames died to a flicker on the waters. The sky cleared in the east and the morning star came out, brilliant before the sun, still hiding below the horizon. As the sun came up, Praeger could see the towers of the city to the south, their glassy facets catching the sun's shout.

He got up and looked around at the stricken forest land in the morning light, patched here and there with new greenery struggling out of the ground and along tree branches. The bridge at his right was a cinder, still slowly collapsing into the river. He decided to make his way along the bank on foot until he found another bridge where he could cross to the other side and return to the city.

Parks of Rest and Culture

THE air was foul, barely breathable, acceptable only to those who had no choice. The pool, five hundred feet long and two hundred wide, was almost completely hidden in the predawn darkness. It had once been operational, but now all the pavement was cracked and huge stones sat on the empty bottom; they had rolled down from the cliffs which rose in a semicircle at the west end of the grounds. The single granite and concrete module which had been the administration building sat on its own concrete island in the center of the waterless pool. Inside, the two floors had partially caved in. On its high granite pillar on the roof the old clock was dead at two A.M.—or P.M. The whole area had once been a park, but now the branches on the trees outside the fence were bare and brittle and dry.

Beyond the tall fence, above the dead trees, the lights from the stone city penetrated weakly through the layers of dirt-fog and morning mists. There stood the old apartment buildings which were not serviced by the numerous air filtration plants scattered throughout the city.

Praeger stood in the metal doorway of the main filter house and peered at the soft grained lights beyond the fence through his air filter mask. The face-plate sprouted a spiral hose which ended in the chemical tank strapped to his chest. At his feet he felt the vibrations of the huge pumps below ground which filtered the air, heated or cooled it for those select New York City buildings whose tenants qualified for the utility and pre-service modifications under the Human Resources Allocations Act of 1985. Such buildings had no windows, only locks at the front entrance, seldom used; each roof was a copter square.

This morning, when his night shift was over, he would have to take the subway home; the city copter was out of service. He tried to accept the thought and ignore it.

He peered up past the fence and eroded hillside through his faceplate and thought of the eyes which would be watching him as it grew lighter, when he left the grounds through the gate.

He looked to the east, where the orbital space mirror was hastening the dawn by two hours, to light up the city early with its reflected light; an effort to keep crime down. On the Asian mainland, he knew, the Russians were using similar mirrors to light up their battlefields with the Chinese.

The real dawn was more than an hour away. Praeger turned and walked back inside the open doorway. He did not bother taking off his mask inside.

The plant hummed, and after a few moments the humming seemed to become a roar as the vibrating air pressed in on his ears. He walked down the row of pressure gauges, giving each one a glance. Then he went to the log pad on the wall and filled in the data. He could have done it without checking; the figures were always the same.

He went outside again as if hoping for something miraculous to happen. He stood in the open door, leaning against the metal frame and looking toward downtown—mid-Manhattan, where he could just barely see the old trade center towering over the Empire State Building, a pair of titans against the steel-gray sky. Always, he thought, the old and the new, the old never quite dying away, the dream never replacing the reality entirely. When we start for Centauri, there will still be mud huts in Asia, the unclean washing away their sins in the Ganges.

In the eastern sky an eye opened in the morning mists, a white-hot reflecting surface shouting the sun's light earthward.

Praeger waited, and later came the true dawn; incredibly scarlet, a function of all the dirt in earth's atmosphere, it streaked the sky. The planet could still manage its own kind of beauty. Though the wounds of the biosphere were deep, they were healing into scars. But the thin layer of human consciousness stretched over the surface of the planet—the noösphere—had ruptured; and the human organism in its entirety was being spilled back into the evolutionary past, into the abyss of screams.

In the morning sunlight the concrete surfaces of the pool area were a bright gray-white. Praeger began his walk around the fence on the inside, checking for damage; a human insect moving slowly on the slightly raised walk.

At the west end of the grounds, just below the cliffs, he found a large hole in the chain fence, the largest of six during the week. It led to the small path that ran on the other side of the fence just below the cliff wall. It was not a planned path, but one which had been created by vandals, prowlers and playing children during the years. He smiled, thinking, they have better wire cutters than the city repair crews. The hole was very neatly cut out. He turned away from the fence toward the administration building and walked briskly across.

He stopped in front of the flagpole by the front entrance, noticing that the rope had been cut again during the night. Then he went into the small office, the only usable room in the empty building, and found that the night watchman had vomited all over the floor again.

The place stank, but he forced himself to sign the blotter and punch out on the creaky old machine. The watchman, as usual, had checked out hours ago, knowing that no one would report him, or care.

Praeger went over to the crusty old bulletin board and peered at the new addition. The examination to renew his technician's rating was to be given at 1:00 P.M., May 1, 1998, which was next Wednesday. He was worried about the rising standards and about his wife's reaction if he did not pass. Would she accept living in a non-environmental-control apartment—one open to the air, with perhaps only an air conditioner for the summer? They had adjusted well to seeing each other only in the afternoons, but she would never be—had never been—very close to him. He did not know what she would do.

He left the office and went along the walk by the fence until he came to the north exit gate, his shadow a long darkness to his right. Here once huge crowds of people had stood in line to gain entrance to the pool. He fumbled with the key and opened the rusty old lock; he pushed at the gate, straining, until it creaked open enough for him to pass. He locked it behind him and paused at the top of the stone steps which led to the street below.

Across the street stood red-brick apartment buildings, five stories each, open-windowed, unserviced by the plant in which he worked. A number of the people who lived in these buildings were hired every month during the backblowing operation at the plant—the process by which the huge filters were removed and cleaned. Usually that was done on his shift and he supervised it with the help of two armed policemen.

He heard a clatter on the step pavement near him. A half-dozen stones struck and bounced and rolled around him. He looked up in time to see the kids on the roof of the house directly in front of him duck away from his masked gaze. He went down the steps and walked north along the street toward the Tremont subway station. He felt slightly relieved when he came to the big police cruiser parked next to a fire hydrant. Inside, the uniformed policemen were asleep in air-conditioned comfort. He stopped and rapped with his knuckles on the heavy safety plastic "glass." One of the cops woke up, looked at the dash clock, grinned and waved his thanks as Praeger turned to continue down the street. In a moment the cruiser turned on its engines and air system to high and streaked past him on its way to the precinct. As he watched it disappear ahead of him, he could almost feel the eagerness of the two cops to get to the station to check out. Momentarily he felt a keen resentment because the copter had not come to pick him up. Normally he would have been halfway home by now.

There was an old man staggering toward him down the street with one hand outstretched. "Money?" the old man said, stopping in front of him, blocking his way. The thought of the old man's mouth so near him, the mouth and nose taking in air in greedy gasps, the chest rising and falling in seeming panic, made Praeger sick. The old man's body was shaking; the effort he was exerting to control his stance resulted in a powerful sustained trembling. The eyes were bloodshot; one was set crookedly in its socket and seemed to be staring at the pavement.

Praeger shook his head. He never carried any money with him. His green city uniform would be enough to admit him to the subway.

"None left? No more—no more money?" the old man rasped in amazement. He coughed. Then his good eye also turned down to look at the pavement and he dragged himself past Praeger, as if resigned to the fact that there was nothing to be gained from this astonishing masked creature.

Praeger continued down the street. He turned the corner and went up the hill to Tremont. At the top of the hill there was a small park. Here, too, the trees were dead. There were no squirrels or birds, but a lone cockroach darted past him into the sewer. He remembered, years ago, sitting in St. James Park—on a bench, looking into the cracked and gullied clay tennis courts—watching the pigeons and squirrels moving around in the meager grass. There had even been leaves on many of the trees in those days, enough to hide the tall tower of the bank which held the Fordham clock. Then the Jerome Avenue elevated train had come by, noisier every year as the foliage diminished. It had scared the shit out of all the animals. Every year there had been more dead birds and squirrels lying around. Then, one year, there was no spring.

She came into the room and sat down on the bed where he was sleeping. "Did you hear me, Chris?" There was no urgency in her voice. He mumbled and tried to turn over but she was sitting on the covers.

"The milkman brought an extra bottle of water today by mistake, didn't you notice? I'm not going to tell him."

"Betty, let me sleep." He tried to turn over but she was still in the way. She started rubbing his stomach, to arouse him. He had been dreaming of working on a space station. . . .

He opened his eyes and looked at her. She had that usual blank look on her face, the one she wore when she wasn't angry or dreaming. Her long blond hair was combed out and she had nothing on. The daylights were on in the room. The landscape wall showed the mountain valley in Canada where she had been born. He thought of all the power she used keeping the wall on, and how little of her salary as a daycare instructor she used for the apartment.

"Betty, please get out of here and let me sleep."

"When is your exam?"

"Next Wednesday, now get out!"

She smiled and walked out of the room. The daylights and picture wall went out as she closed the door. In a moment he knew she would be dialing someone on the phone. He became drowsy again, wrapping himself in the darkness. The space station was in front of him, a jeweled toy next to a sparkling earth.

He came into the lobby, his air mask under his left arm, and stopped under the huge glass chandelier. There was no point in worrying about the examination, he told himself. It would soon be done and over with. A large sign on the wall to his left caught his eye. He walked up to it and read the print below the huge photograph of the earth in space. The legend urged him to take a job on one of the trans-lunar-earth stations tied in with ecosystem and resource control.

There was a list of openings—weatherwatch, atmospheric engineering, satellite repair, orbital debris clearance. The requirements were: a technical background and aptitude, and the capacity to work alone. Benefits included generous earth leaves, and further opportunities to work in extra-lunar and moon surface positions. Applications here at Central Park West Station. The wall view poster bore the name NASA-EUROSOV.

The NASA-EUROSOV office was just down the hall from the wall view poster. Praeger walked in, picked up an application from the dispenser and filled in his tech identification number. He waited a few minutes, knowing that it was now too late to get to his examination room, and dropped the computer card into the receiving slot on his way out. His tech rating could not expire before he qualified for the NASA-EUROSOV programs, which usually had to go begging for applicants.

In the hallway he thought of the disadvantages of working in space, all the little things which made it impossible for a man to do it for any great time. Physical and mental disadvantages. The moon was better, if a man made up his mind to stay for good. Otherwise he would have to wear special weights during his stay to keep him in shape for earthside. It was easy, they said, to put off wearing them.

He came into the lobby again and looked up at the twenty-four-hour clock on the wall. It was four in the afternoon. He had four hours before he had to be at the air plant. He went to the nearest exit which led to a sub-park shuttle and boarded a car for the museum. There he wandered around the great halls feeling somewhat lost until it was time to leave for work. He waited until the last possible moment, then put on his mask and boarded the elevator which would take him to the street lock.

There was a stillness in the waiting. The moon was a white disk over the empty pool, riding low toward the morning. Praeger stood looking up at it through his faceplate, waiting to go off shift. Around the moon he saw the clouds which would cover it before it set.

On the other side of the moon, he knew, the Russians had built a grand hotel for their scientists and moon personnel, a huge structure with gardens and fountains, where the air was very much like that of Odessa in the 1880s. It was rumored that the Russians were mining the first discovered deposits of moon ice, and bottling some of it as a special mineral water for their more credulous countrymen. The "hotel" was really the living quarters of the large science city located in Tsiolkovsky Crater. He had heard stories of beautiful interiors, filled with red carpets and paintings, grand banquet halls and shiny brass railings, where aging Soviet leaders would go to spend their "longer years" in the one-sixth gravity. The science city itself was devoted to physics and biology and astronomy— generally to the exploitation of conditions which were unique for a variety of research programs. Even the aging bureaucrats could be made useful by entering them as case histories in various medical programs. The educated elite who lived there breathed perfect air; for them the Marxist dream of parks of rest and culture had been fulfilled; for them and those like them, technological men and scientists, would come all the fruits of knowledge, perhaps even immortality. To live on the moon required all the planning and care which had been denied to those on earth, and which was being given to the home world very late; but for those who had lived on the moon for many years and would never come back, perhaps raise sons there, the bitter native land which was earth was too beautiful in the sky to be in need of help. The American science city was less stylish, more cool and professional, but essentially the same.

On earth one generation of the overgrown organism which was humanity would have to die off to make the population manageable again. Praeger wondered about the plague proposal made a while ago. A good plague, they had said, would leave everything standing, and mankind would have a chance to get itself back on the right path. Better than a war. Anyway, some would make it, he thought. He wondered about the long-term good of it, and the short-term evil; and the ones who would not understand, the ones who would die to create the compost for the future.

Clouds obscured the moon and he thought, somehow . . . we men . . . were on the way to becoming fully ourselves just a little while ago, getting a grip on ourselves and reality; then we made some horrible mistake which kept us from passing that threshold into becoming something . . . new . . .

He stopped thinking and went back inside the plant to take his readings. Someday, he hoped, children would look back at this time as the great depression of the '90s . . . what year would be the cutoff point?

The apartment was quiet when he woke up that afternoon. He strained to hear Betty in the kitchen, but there was no sound. Maybe she was sitting at the table sipping coffee? He turned over and looked at her bed. It was neatly made and empty, a dark mass in the faint nightlight.

He got up slowly and stretched, went to the door, opened it, and took three strides to reach the bathroom. He found her note taped to the medicine cabinet mirror. It read: "I left you a message on the recorder." It was written in big black letters.

He turned and went out into the living room, turning the daylights on with his presence. He walked over to the green sofa and sat down, staring at the recorder on the coffee table. As he turned it on, he heard the front door open and close. He pushed the play button and looked at himself in the large mirror sitting in his pajamas. Behind him Betty came into the room.

"Chris, understand—" her voice on the tape started to say.

"Turn it off," Betty said in the mirror. He watched her in the glass. She was dressed in a green raincoat cut to look like a jacket and skirt.

"—what I'm going to tell you." He stabbed at the off button.

"I didn't want you sitting around like an orphan listening to a voice on a tape," she said. "I want to tell you myself—I owe you that much."

He wasn't going to speak to her, no matter how much he wanted to.

"I'm leaving, Chris. You're not going to make much more of yourself, you'll start to slip and we'll wind up in open housing. I'll look great when I'm wheezing and bald. I'm not going to sit around and wait for it."

He was silent, wishing she would just go.

"You're going to blame me now, aren't you?"

He shook his head suddenly, *no,* hoping that she would say it and be finished. There was a trembling in his insides. He felt as if he were in a trance which she would break with her next words.

"There's someone else and he can help me get what I want—everything we'll both ever want . . ."

He looked directly at her for a moment and saw that her lower lip was shaking. Her face was a frightening thing; it repelled him and he looked away. He began to rub his eyes with his hands. She turned and left the room. He heard the front door shut itself automatically behind her. He felt his face become drawn and he felt a great warmth surround his consciousness, as if the room were becoming a furnace; and he heard the sound of his pulse in his ears, the blood pounding behind his eyes.

It began to rain in the late afternoon and continued all night. Toward morning there were huge puddles of water in the empty pool at the air plant. The metal door to the inside jammed and

Praeger had to leave it open and wear his mask all night. In the morning he took a chair and sat in the doorway watching the rain come down in the gloom, beating on the pavement. Thousands of hurrying rivulets ran on the concrete and cascaded into the empty pool. The sound of the water relaxed him. He thought of the empty apartment waiting for him, and felt the tiredness creeping into his body. He looked forward to the oblivion of sleep.

Today also the helicopter would not come for him; he was no longer worth the effort, he thought. He was leaving at the end of the week; the copter fuel was more valuable to them.

Just before he had left for work, notification had come from NASA-EUROSOV through the mail readout slot telling him they had a job for him on one of the earth-moon sector stations. He was to settle his affairs and vacate his apartment. There had been a word of congratulations on the print-out, and a note asking him if he would waive minimum earth leave for higher pay.

As a NASA-EUROSOV employee he had regained the right to have children, indirectly, by depositing his sperm; a right which Betty had convinced him to sell. But the sperm bank was a good bet against the future. He had heard of illegal children being readied for a new earth swept clean by deliberate plague; children hidden away throughout the solar system. Somewhere, he was sure, men were preparing for the stars. He dreamed of unspoiled earths around far suns, wondering how long it would be before the stardrive breakthrough changed the world and if he would be part of it.

He went off shift and walked up the hill to the Tremont station. The rain ran down his Pyrex faceplate. He wore no hat and his hair was wet. His clothing was waterproof. He tightened his collar to keep the water from running inside. The rain seemed to be coming down harder than before and he could not see very far ahead. He needed a windshield wiper, like the big blades on the police cruiser. The thought tickled him—sweep, sweep! He couldn't see it but he could feel it: the water was high around his boots as it ran down the hill.

Two men grabbed his arms and twisted them behind his back and a third ripped off his air mask, chest tank and all. They pushed him on his back with his head downhill and in a moment they vanished again in the thick curtain of rain.

He got up breathing hard and coughing. The air was heavy and wet in his lungs and he felt nauseous. His wrists seemed sprained. His face was streaming. Water ran in his eyes, blinding him. He screamed and shook both his fists in the rain; the gesture hurt, and the sound was lost against the rush of water in his ears. His eyes began to hurt and he rubbed them, cursing silently now. Then he walked the remaining half block to the subway entrance, coughing without letup all the way.

The entrance was a gaping black hole leading down into the earth, surrounded by a wilderness of rain. On the platform he took out a handkerchief and tied it around his face.

On the train going uptown he knew the other passengers were all staring at him, secretly pleased that he had lost his mask; but when he confronted their eyes they seemed to lose interest in him. He wondered, did NASA-EUROSOV know about Betty leaving him? Was that why they had mentioned the e-visitation clause, knowing that he would have no immediate ties on earth? If she had started the divorce action, then central information—CENTIN—would have it in his file, which could have been already tapped by NASA-EUROSOV. He could check it, but it didn't really matter. The sperm deposit. That, too. If he had gone in to be sterilized, they would have given him money, just like for blood, just like they had sold their right to have kids. But now they would put his sperm in a bank, with the eventual certainty that it would be used. Someone was making all possible bets against the future, making sure that as many different combinations were at least available as possible. It was being used as a kind of incentive to go along with his new job, he was sure of it.

He thought of the stories he had heard of hidden groups of children belonging to high officials on earth or on the moon, children being readied for a new earth, maybe even the stars? He hoped, perhaps something will happen and we'll get a stardrive in my lifetime, and if I'm out there working when it happens maybe I'll get in on it! He felt a wild surge of expectation at the thought, a momentary release from the dark prison of his puny self.

The train reached his station and delivered him into the drenching rain and acrid air, again.

• • •

At the end of the week he closed the apartment and took a jet to Nevada, where the whip catapult serving the earth stations was located. The desert conjured up visions of the sun domes on Mars, green plants growing lush in low gravity, filling the bright space of the dome with oxygen. He did not have to wear a mask here, in Nevada, where the helicopter had left him off. What of Mars, where the desert bloomed . . . what of earthlike planets around far suns, unspoiled! How soon, he wondered, will we make the crucial breakthrough which will save us—tip the balance in favor of our dreams? A gust of wind came up from nowhere and blew some sand in his face and made his eyes water.

The spaceport was surrounded by a city of trailers and cabins. They gave him a cabin with a skylight for the one day before his departure for earth station one. He lay resting, and then dreaming, in the stillness of half sleep, of sun over treetops, an uncancerous sun, setting; a sliver of daylight moon; sky deep blue; evening star blazing; wind on the tall grass; shadows of clouds; last spring with no sound in the air . . .

The last real spring he had known had been in Central Park, years ago. The water of the small lake had been a green mirror, and the white swan had sailed curve-necked toward where the willows washed their branches in the water . . .

Tomorrow he would be on the shuttle.

The earth was blue-green below as he thought of yesterday's thought of being here now. Acceleration was over and he leaned weightless in his straps toward the porthole, knowing that the stars and moon would look clearer now than from earth, that bottom of a dirty ocean where he had been born. It was a clean break now. Sunlight flooded the shuttlecraft like a shout. He floated back in his seat and tightened the straps, and dreamed of a healed earth as it might still be, one hundred . . . five hundred . . . years hence, free of its billions and the guilty minority responsible for a century of plunder.

He dreamed he saw parks of rest and culture filled with elegant people, full-leafed trees casting broad shadows; and at night stars would be looking down, bright lights in an empty hall above an earth abandoned by most of its people.

The Water Sculptor

Sitting there, watching the Earth below him from the panel of Station Six, Christian Praeger suddenly felt embarrassed by the planet's beauty. For the last eight hours he had watched the great storm develop in the Pacific, and he had wanted to share the view with someone, tell someone how beautiful he thought it was. He had told it to himself now for the fiftieth time.

The storm was a physical evil, a spinning hell that might with luck reach the Asian mainland and kill thousands of starving billions. They would get a warning, for all the good that would do. Since the turn of the century there had been dozens of such storms, developing in places way off from the traditional storm cradles.

He looked at the delicate pinwheel. It was a part of the planet's ecology—whatever state that was in now. The arms of the storm reminded him of the theory which held the galaxy to be a kind of organized storm system which sucked in gas and dust at its center and sent it all out into the vast arms to condense into stars. And the stars were stormy laboratories building the stuff of the universe in the direction of huge molecules, from the inanimate and crystalline to the living and conscious. In the slowness of time it all looked stable, Praeger thought, but almost certainly all storms run down and die.

He looked at the clock above the center screen. There were six clocks around the watch room, one above each screen. The clock on the ceiling gave station time. His watch would be over in half an hour.

He looked at the sun screen. There all the dangerous rays were filtered out. He turned up the electronic magnification and for a long time watched the prominences flare up and die. He looked at the cancerous sunspots. The sight was hypnotic and frightening no matter how many times he had seen it. He put his hand out to the computer panel and punched in the routine information. Then he looked at the spectroscopic screens, small rectangles beneath the earth watch monitors. He checked the time, and set the automatic release for the ozone scatter-cannisters to be dropped into the atmosphere. A few minutes later he watched them drop away from the station, following their fall until they broke in the upper atmosphere, releasing the precious ozone that would protect Earth's masses from the sun's deadly radiation. Early in the twentieth century a good deal of the natural ozone layer in the upper atmosphere had been stripped away as a result of atomic testing and the use of aerosol sprays, resulting in much genetic damage in the late eighties and nineties. But soon now the ozone layer would be back up to snuff.

When his watch ended ten minutes later, Praeger was glad to get away from the visual barrage of the screens. He made his way into one of the jutting spokes of the station where his sleep cubicle was located. Here it was a comfortable half-g all the time. He settled himself into his bunk, and pushed the music button at his side, leaving his small observation and com screen on the ceiling turned off. Gradually the music filled the room and he closed his eyes. Mahler's weary song of earth's misery enveloped his consciousness with pity and weariness, and love. Before he fell asleep he wished he might feel the earth's atmosphere the way he felt his own skin.

I wish I could hear and feel the motion of gas molecules in the upper air, the whisperings of subtle energy transfers . . .

In the Pacific, weather control engineers guided the great storm into an electrostatic basket. The storm would provide usable power for the rest of its natural life.

• • •

Praeger awoke a quarter of an hour before his watch was due to begin. He thought of his recent vacation earthside, remembering the glowing volcano he had seen in Italy, and how strange the silver shield of the Moon had looked from behind all the atmosphere. He remembered watching his own station six, his post in life, moving slowly across the sky; remembered one of the inner stations as it passed Julian's station 233, one of the few private satellites, synchronous, fixed for all time over one point on the Earth. He should be able to talk to Julian soon, during his next off period. Even though Julian was an artist and a recluse, a water sculptor as he called himself, Julian and he were very much alike. At times he felt they were each other's conscience, two ex-spacemen in continual retreat from their home world. It was much more beautiful, and bearable from out here. In all this silence he sometimes thought he could hear the universe breathing. It was alive, the whole starry cosmos throbbing.

If I could tear a hole in its body, it would bleed and cry out for a Band-aid . . .

He remembered the stifling milieu of Rome's streets: the great screens which went dead during his vacation, blinding the city, the crowds waiting on the stainless steel squares for the music to resume over the giant audios. They could not work without it. The music pounded its monotonous bass beat: the sound of some imprisoned beast beneath the city. The cab that waited for him was a welcome sight: an instrument for fleeing.

In the shuttle craft that brought him back to station six he read the little quotation printed on the back of every seat for the 10,000th time; it told him that the shuttle dated back to the building of the giant earth station system.

". . . What we are building now is the nervous system of mankind . . . the communications network of which the satellites will be the nodal points. They will enable the consciousness of our grandchildren to flicker like lightning back and forth across the face of the planet . . ."

Praeger got up from his bunk and made his way back to the watch room. He was glad now to get away from his own thoughts and return to the visual stimulation of the watch screens. Soon he would be talking to Julian again; they would share each other's friendship in the universe of the spoken word as they shared a silent past every time they looked at each other across the void.

Julian's large green eyes reminded him each time of the view out by Neptune, the awesome size of the sea green giant, the ship outlined against it, and the fuel tank near it blossoming into a red rose, silently; the first ship had been torn in half. Julian had been in space, coming over to Praeger's command ship when it happened, to pick up a spare part for the radio-telescope. *They* blamed Julian because *they* had to blame some-one. After all, he had been in command. Chances were that something had already gone wrong, and that nothing could have stopped it. Only one man had been lost.

Julian and Praeger were barred from taking any more mis-sions, unfairly, they thought. There were none coming up that either of them would have been interested in anyway, but at the time they put up a fight. Some fool official said publicly that they were unfit to represent mankind beyond the solar system—a silly thing to say, especially when the UN had just put a ban on extra-solar activities. They were threatened with dishonorable discharges, but they were world heroes; the pub-licity would have been embarrassing.

Julian believed that most of mankind was unfit for just about everything. With his small fortune and the backing of patrons he built his bubble station, number 233 in the registry; his occupation now was "sculptor," and the tax people came to talk to him every year. To Julian Earth was a mudball, where ten per cent of the people lived off the labor of the other ninety percent. Oh, the brave ones shine, he told Praeger once, but the initiative that should have taken men to the stars had been ripped out of men's hearts. The whole star system was rotting, overblown with grasping things living in their own wastes. The promise of ancient myths, three thousand years old, had not been fulfilled . . .

In the watch room Praeger watched the delicate clouds which enveloped the earth. He could feel the silence, and the slowness of the changing patterns was reassuring. Given time and left alone, the air would clean itself of all man-made wastes, the rivers would run clear again, and the oceans would regain their abundance of living things.

When his watch was over he did not wait for his relief to come. He didn't like the man. The feeling was mutual and by leaving early they could each avoid the other as much as was possible. Praeger went directly to his cubicle, lay down on his bunk, and opened the channel, both audio and visual, on the ceiling com and observation screen.

Julian's face came on promptly on the hour.

"EW-CX233 here," Julian said.

"EW-CX006," Praeger said. Julian looked his usual pale self, green eyes with the look of other times still in them. "Hello, Julian. What have you been doing?"

"There was a reporter here. I made a tape of the whole thing, if you can call it an interview. Want to hear it?"

"Go ahead. My vacation was the usual. I don't know what's wrong with me."

Julian's face disappeared and the expressionless face of the reporter appeared. The face smiled just before it spoke.

"Julian—that's the name you are known by?"

"Yes."

"Will you describe your work for our viewers, Julian?"

"I am a water sculptor. I make thin plastic molds and fill them with water. Then I put them out into the void and when they solidify I go out and strip off the plastic. You can see most of my work orbiting my home."

"Isn't the use of water expensive?"

"I re-use much of it. And I am independently wealthy."

"What's the point of leaving your work outside?"

"On Earth the wind shapes rock. Here space dust shapes the ice, mutilates it, and I get the effect I want. Then I photograph the results in color, and make more permanent versions here inside."

Praeger watched Julian and the reporter float over to a large tank of water.

"Inside here," Julian said, "you see the permanent figures. When I spin the tank the density of each becomes apparent, and each takes its proper place in the suspension."

"Do you ever work with realistic subjects?"

"No."

"Do you think you could make a likeness of the Earth?"

"Why?" Praeger saw Julian smile politely. The reporter suddenly looked uncomfortable. The tape ended and Julian's face appeared.

"See what they send up here to torment me?"

"Is the interview going to be used anywhere?" Praeger asked.

"They were vague about it."

"Have you been happy?"

Julian didn't answer. For a few moments both screens were still portraits. Both men knew all the old complaints, all the old pains. Both knew that the UN was doing secret extra-solar work, and they both knew that it was the kind of work that would revive them, just as it might give the Earth a new lease on life. But they would never have a share of it. Only a few more years of routine service, Praeger knew, and then retirement—to what? To a crowded planet.

Both men thought the same thought at that moment—the promise of space was dead, unless men moved from the solar system.

"Julian," Praeger said softly, "I'll call you after my next watch." Julian nodded and the screen turned gray.

On impulse Praeger pushed the observation button for a look at station 233. It was a steel and plastic ball one hundred feet in diameter. Praeger knew that most of Julian's belongings floated in the empty center, tied together with line. When he needed something he would bounce around the tiny universe of objects until he found it. Some parts of the station were transparent. Praeger remembered peering out once to catch sight of one of Julian's ice sculptures. He saw a pale white ghost peering in back at him for a moment, and then passing.

Praeger watched the silent ball that housed his friend of a lifetime. Eventually, he knew, he would join Julian in his retirement. A man could live a long time in zero-g.

The alarm in his cubicle rang and Higgins's voice came over the audio. "That fool! Doesn't he see that orbital debris?"

Praeger had perhaps ten seconds left to see station 233 whole. The orbital junk hit hard and the air was gone into the void. The water inside, Praeger knew, froze instantly. Somewhere inside the ruptured body of Julian floated among his possessions even as the lights on the station winked out.

Praeger was getting into his suit, knowing there was no chance to save Julian. He made his way down the emergency passage from his cubicle, futilely dragging the spare suit behind him.

The airlock took an age to cycle. When it opened he gave a great kick with his feet and launched himself out toward the other station. Slowly it grew in front of him, until he was at the airlock. He activated the mechanism and when the locks were both open he pushed himself in toward the center of the little world.

Starlight illuminated Julian's white, ruptured face. Through the clear portion of the station Praeger saw the earth's shadow eclipse the full moon: a bronze shield.

For a long time after Praeger drifted in the starlit shell. He stared at the dark side of the earth, at the cities sparkling like fireflies; never sleeping, billions living in metal caves; keeping time with the twenty-four hour workday; and where by night the mannequins danced beneath the flickering screens, their blood filled with strange potions which would give them their small share of counterfeit happiness.

Praeger tried to brush away the tears floating inside his helmet, but with no success. They would have to wait until he took his suit off. When the emergency crew arrived an hour later, he took charge.

The station was a hazard now and would have to be removed. He agreed. All this would be a funeral rite for Julian, he thought, and he was sure the artist would approve.

He removed all of Julian's written material and sent it down to his publishers, then put Julian's body in a plastic sack and secured it to the north pole of the station bubble.

He left the sculptures inside. On the body Praeger found a small note:

When we grow up we'll see the Earth not as a special place, just one place. Then home will be the starry cosmos. Of course this has always been the case. It is we who will have changed. I have nothing else to hope for.

The hulk continued in its orbit for three weeks, until Praeger sent a demolition crew out to it and blew it out of existence. He watched on the monitor as they set the charges that would send it into a new orbit. Station 233 would leave the solar system at an almost ninety degree angle to the plane of the ecliptic, on a parabolic path which would not bring it back to Sol for thousands of years. It would be a comet someday, Praeger thought.

He watched the charges flare up, burn for thirty seconds, and die. Slowly the bubble moved off toward the top of the screen. He watched it until it disappeared from the screen. In twenty-four hours it would be beyond the boundaries of Earth. Interstellar gas and dust would scar it out of all recognition: a seed on the wind.

Rope of Glass

SAM Brickner was halfway down the block, walking slowly to his apartment building on the corner, when the diagnostic van rolled past him and slowed down.

Sam stopped. The light on the corner turned red, a small porthole into hell. The van was standing behind a food ration truck, directly in front of the entrance to his house. He had the sudden fear that they were waiting for him to come near enough so they could force him inside where the medics could take his blood count. He tensed and waited, knowing that it was a long light. He looked at the scratched paint on the rear doors, fearing that his luck was over and they would find out. A muscle near his knee twitched nervously, and he felt his face tighten into a rigid grimace; sweat began to form on his brow.

The light turned green and the medical van moved away. He walked the rest of the way home shaken, feeling as if he had just crossed a glass tightrope and miraculously it had not shattered.

He paused outside the front door to his building. The air of the city was oppressive, a mass composed of exhalations from a billion human throats and the wastes from inhuman machine processes. Sam went inside and up the creaky wooden stairs to the second floor. He opened the old latchlock to his apartment

47

with a key and stepped inside. He closed the door, pushed in all the bolts, and lay down on the large bed in the center of the room. He was still shaking a little.

He tried to calm himself. It had been nothing, he told himself. No one was after him. The man who had jostled him in the crowdjam on 34th Street was a nobody—despite the fact that he had run into him again at the hospital last night. He was probably a subnormal janitor tunnel worker for the New York Hospital complex. The man had shown no sign of recognition when Sam had come out of Katherine's makeshift treatment room in the branch of the hospital's underground transfer tunnel. Kathy would have known if he were a euthanasia cop, but she had told him that the man was an orderly in the hospital, probably on an errand.

Kathy loved him. She loved him despite his age, Sam knew that, because he made her feel like a human being and not a trapped animal. They had their own world together, at least once a month, the uncrowded, unregulated world of each other's presence. She loved him enough to risk saving his life, believing with him that the bootleg Poly-IC drug would in time induce a permanent remission of his body's mimic-leukemia. Twice the drug had almost succeeded, boosting the percent of healthy cells in his bone marrow, running the hemoglobin count in his blood to supernormal levels, making him feel twenty years younger than his fifty-three years. But the bad cells had come back and Katherine had put him through a new series of treatments. "Sam, you've got to hang on," she had said, "it may be a matter of just waiting long enough. The remissions are lasting longer." She had pleaded with him, trying to coax him out of his depression, using words and looks, her body, and all the bootleg drugs and knowledge she could steal for him as a nurse and paramedic.

They would have their years of happiness. She had promised him that, for as long as he lived. He was safe with her; she was the one person who would never turn him in to the death cops. She could not do it without revealing herself as an accomplice in concealing a chronic disease. They would take her life and his for that. She was silent because she loved him.

Calmer now, he fell asleep.

• • •

The man with the flamethrower aimed it at him. The fire leaped out, burning his face, melting his eyes and flesh, scorching the bones of his skull, purging him of all infection.

Sam woke up with the sun in his face, shining at him through the hole in the dirty window shade, warm and blinding. He got up and staggered into the bathroom. His face was pale in the mirror. He looked at it carefully, searching for signs of last night's fear. I have to see real dangers, he told himself as he took off the clothes he had slept in, and not torture myself with imagined ones. I found out soon enough to save my life and justify my existence. I do my job with no trouble. I'm useful. No one complains about me. I am not unfit. No one can tell the difference from day to day, not even the law. And I'm going to get better, maybe even next week. They'll never know what I had, not even after I'm dead.

He took a quick sponge bath in the shower stall with his saved water ration. After shaving he had enough water left for two cups of coffee. Before going out, he took a look at himself in the long mirror on the back of his front door. His hair was thick and black and streaked with gray. His green city worker's uniform was neatly pressed, and the buckle on his black belt was still shiny. He felt reassured by the sight of himself, and he felt definitely stronger after the previous day's Poly-IC treatment.

He opened the door and went down the stairs. On the sidewalk he looked around and saw no crowdjams yet at any of the corners, although traffic in the street was increasing.

He started walking toward the food ration center where he worked, four blocks down-city. As he walked the noise grew louder around him and people began to fill up the sidewalk from the doorways of the apartment buildings. By the time he reached the center ten minutes later, he was walking slowly behind a mass of humanity at least a mile long, each person moving forward at the same time to avoid a jam. He cut out of the crowd and went inside the ration center and up to the second floor where his office was a desk between two partitions on a balcony overlooking the huge warehouse floor below.

He sat down at his desk and stared down into the huge floor

area where endless lines of humanity had stood for more than thirty years of his life while he kept records and checked shipping orders, occasionally catching a counterfeit ration ticket and sending it up to the third floor to the men he had never seen. The only contact he had with them was through the intercom and the air tube which carried papers between floors.

Two years ago Katherine O'Faolian's name had appeared on a counterfeit ration ticket. He had looked up from his desk and had seen her staring up at him, her eyes pleading. The look on her face had been one of unexpected horror. He had picked her out from all the thousands of people on the floor, and it had seemed obvious to him that she had signed the ticket unknowingly. He had torn it up in her sight and had sent down a blank form to replace it.

After work he had found her waiting for him by the front entrance. She had gone home with him, holding him up with her arm when he stumbled along the way. He had been right, he had told himself later; he could not have lived with the thought of her becoming a subnormal laborer for passing the ration ticket. The world lived by rigid rules of productivity, and it was anxious to use up human beings completely.

He remembered the night she had come to his apartment in the middle of winter to find him sick and weak. He remembered a small woman with brown hair and blue eyes wearing a nurse's uniform. As she had leaned over him, he had noticed how pale her face had seemed, making her freckles more prominent than he had ever seen them. Later that night she had brought a doctor to him, and had covered his face while he was being examined and diagnosed, and he had wondered if that was to protect him or the doctor. He had never found out whether the doctor had been a legal practitioner or not.

He remembered how gently she had told him what he had a few days later. It had become fairly common recently: a mimic-leukemia, something which could start like a cancer of the blood, disappear suddenly and return just as unexpectedly to kill the marrow's capacity to make fresh blood cells. The Poly-IC drug could prod the bone marrow into new production, and might eventually stimulate the organism into a complete remission, but he had to have intravenous doses of the stuff whenever his healthy cell count went down. The drug's side effects were flu symptoms, high temperature, and severe shivering during the treatment, but they went away in reasonable time.

He had avoided the end, but complete remission had not taken place. The world wanted him to die. There were too many human cells to make a healthy humanity; failing cells had to be flushed out of the organism. In one or two generations the patient might begin to live again.

Sam sat up straight in his chair and picked up a pen from his desk. He picked up the first sheet of paper from the pile in front of him and tried to read it, but his eyes wandered to look out through the glass instead. A line was forming by the first trough below; workers dressed in green coveralls were coming in to dispense the day's first rations. Suddenly Sam was looking at the same man who had jostled him in the crowd-jam and whom he had seen at the hospital. The man was staring up at him blatantly, deliberately torturing him with his presence. Sam tried to look as if he were doing his job, but his eyes refused to limit their attention to the paper on his desk. The man continued to stare at him. Sam knew the man was sensing his fear, and when he smiled at him Sam almost cried out inside, sure that the other's gaze had penetrated into him and had seen everything.

He knows, Sam said to himself; but I won't lead them to you, Kathy. He hid his sweat-covered face with his hand, hoping that somehow he might die right there, that his circulatory system would shatter like glass, spilling his diseased fluids into his body cavities and leaving nothing for his heart to pump. He remembered how strong he had been after the first few treatments. Kathy had been delighted with him, vowing that she would never want anyone else. He remembered the first time he had made love to her and how she had cried out. The sleep he had shared with her then seemed so very precious now, and he wished that he had died in it...

He took his hand away from his face and looked for the stranger below; but the man was no longer looking at him. Suddenly he seemed just an ordinary man waiting passively for his rations to be doled out.

• • •

At four o'clock they put the news on over the building's loudspeakers. Sam tried to ignore it as he checked through some files in the cabinets in the rear of the balcony, but he listened to the last few minutes of the commentator's daily inspirational when he got back to his desk.

". . . and finally I say to all good Americans who want to see a better America—the world is out of control, but *we* have closed our shores, stopped all pollution, cut our population growth to hold steady under two billion this year; our death rate is the highest in the world this year *and* last. And we will have our Horn of Plenty! Our best scientific minds are working day and night to perfect the universal matter synthesizer which will give us anything we want from basic raw materials— anything from a ham sandwich to a chunk of steel. Unlimited fusion power—power to rip matter apart at its basic level and put it back together into anything . . . fusion power and laser scanning of matter to form the image and the reality of a better world, a planet free of the need for agriculture and the tasteless synthetics we eat now. Money and time and mind will free mankind, as long as the research continues, as long as the unfit pass from our midst. Those who cannot serve the future with healthy bodies must contribute by quitting the game. They too are patriots and heroes, here by a mistake of nature or the curse of the past. We must set things right, purging humanity of sickness so it may survive into better times. The Horn of Plenty is just around the corner. We cannot hesitate now and waste all those who have died. Courage . . ."

It was the same speech every day. Only the voices changed. Sam knew it by heart, like he knew the prayers of his childhood. He had grown up at the end of the good times near the turn of the century. He had seen all the good ideas die in their application to life. He had lived through the drug resistant plagues, through the brief reprieves of the 1990s, through the tyranny of the innovations control boards and their stifling of new technologies, through the global depression following the world crop failures. He had seen UN-enforced migrations, culminating in the complete isolationism of the big powers after the pogroms and expulsions. He had been a plumber and electrician, a union official. At fifty-three he held his job in the food ration chain because national employees were never fired. They worked until they died or contracted a disease. He had lived to see his union pension and social security turn into ration tickets. At work he tried to look fit enough to avoid suspicion that might lead to a spot medical check. In many cases old age was defined as a terminal and chronic disease. The death cops could arrest you directly for that, diagnose you at the euthanasia terminal and send you on your way, saving everyone time and money.

But Kathy lived in this world with him, making it bearable. She was there at night when he felt most alone and afraid, and she would never hurt him. She was exactly what he needed her to be. She was for him; for now.

"This way please. Don't worry. It's all arranged. Lie down. Give me your arm."

The straps tightened around his body. The nurse's face fell away and he saw that it wasn't Kathy O'Faolian. It was the face of a death cop, a skull with glass eyes leaning over him, attaching the gas mask to his face and leaving it there, leaving it forever, and nodding back and forth as it turned on the flow of oblivion with white fingers, making him taste the gas in his mouth. He screamed into the mask, gasping the mixture into his lungs . . .

He woke up and Kathy was mopping his face with a cloth. He shivered under the blankets. The empty intravenous bottle hung on its post near the bed.

"How do you feel?" she asked, and smiled.

"Like before," he managed to say. "Maybe—maybe this time will be the last."

She nodded, smiling. Her eyes were so clearly blue in the lights of the small room, so completely without guile or despair, so young.

"I love you," he said and shivered again, so violently this time that he shook the metal bed.

He heard someone take hold of the doorknob and turn it back and forth loudly, followed by a knock on the door.

"In the hall, Kathy, someone's there," Sam said.

She stood up and turned her back to him. He looked up at

her, but the low overhead light blinded him partially. "They've found us, Kathy—who could it be?" She paid no attention to him.

"Open up, Kathy," a voice said from beyond the door; "open up or I'll bring help." Sam knew that he couldn't even get up to defend her; and she didn't seem to care.

She went to the door and opened the lock. Someone pushed the door open, and Sam saw a figure shove Kathy back.

"Harry, how did you find this place?" she asked, and her voice sounded strange to Sam, as if what she was saying was for his benefit and not for the intruder.

The man did not answer. He came over and looked down at him, and Sam recognized the face which had terrified him.

"Old man," Harry said, "I'm going to kill you the easy way. I'm going to turn you in. A thirty-second call is all it will take. They'll never know who did it. Maybe tomorrow morning—"

"Harry, for God's sake please leave!" Kathy said.

The man turned suddenly to face her. Sam heard the silence and then Harry saying, "You dump him and I'll let him live ... Kathy, I love you, I've known you a long—"

And he heard Kathy, his Kathy, whisper back, and he knew she was hoping he wouldn't hear. "Okay, Harry, but go now, I beg you. I'll come to you later for sure, but go now."

In a moment the other man was gone and Sam heard Kathy close the door to the dark hallway. He shivered again, less violently now. He felt like stretching all the muscles of his body in one long motion. "Sam, I'm sorry I'm not what you want me to be," Kathy said somewhere far away. "It was all real between us, everything, believe me." It was all a bad dream. Nothing to worry about. Abruptly there was nothing underneath him. He fell and was slowed to perfect stillness by a liquid sleep.

In the long moment before he woke up he dreamed of soaring birds and swift gazelles leaping against a background of graceful trees. He opened his eyes, losing the clearest sky he had ever seen; but he was left with a sensation of physical well-being that he had not known since his youth. He knew it was the drug, but he could almost believe that this time the remission would be complete.

He sat up and saw that he was alone in the room. He threw off the covers, got up, and had started to put on his pants when the door opened with a key from the outside and Kathy came in wearing her nurse's raincoat.

"Oh, you're up," she said almost coldly.

He finished dressing and sat down on the bed, remembering and waiting for her to speak. He wanted to believe anything that she would say but something inside him was transfixed and screaming.

"I had to go to him," she said, "to save your life. I went while you slept."

He looked up at her. It was someone else speaking to him, not Kathy. "While I slept . . . ?"

She nodded. "Sam, forgive me," she said in a low voice, "but you see I had to do it. It's been going on for a long time, from before I met you, from when he and I first started at the hospital. He says he can't stop . . ."

He looked at her, saw the half-formed tears in her eyes, but no shame. He felt old despite his borrowed health, a survivor from a different world, draining the life from . . . this child with the last kicks of his diseased body. He was lying to her, revealing to her what he wanted her to see of him—the way he was inside under all the old flesh, the way he could never be again. And hiding behind even the youth inside him was an old man, buried deeper than he would admit to himself. That was the person who wanted her, who needed her with the attachment of a jealous child and would do anything to keep her.

He stood up and looked at her, wondering what the two of them said to each other about him. "Who is he, Kathy; where does he live?"

She looked at him and the possibility of tears was gone from her eyes. He came up to her and shook her. "Where does he live, Kathy, what's his name? Choose now, love, do you hear me?"

"What are you going to do?"

"Nothing," he said.

"He's an orderly—Harry Andrews, across the street . . ."

He went past her and out the door. "Sam!" she shouted after him. "Come back. Don't you see it's over with him . . . Sam!"

He ignored her cries and walked down the branch corridor to the main passage which ran up to street level a quarter mile away. There he went through an old door which let him out into an alley in back of the hospital. It was a seldom used exit, and even if anyone noticed him his green uniform would get him by.

He came out into the street from the alley and noticed the old brick apartment building across the street from the hospital, where many of the hospital staff lived for as long as they could hold their jobs. Harry Andrews probably shared rooms with a dozen other men.

Sam crossed the street, feeling a remarkable new lightness in his step. He stopped in front of the entrance to the building and checked the names of the mailbox panel. *Harry Andrews— 4L* was the third name he looked at. He pushed the buzzer and held it until the reply buzzer sounded and he was able to push through the front door. He started quickly up the stairs instead of using the elevator.

He turned around on the third landing and Harry Andrews was standing there staring at him from the next floor. The younger man's surprise quickly turned to a look of contempt. Sam felt the muscles in his own face tighten and tremble slightly.

"Now what's this, old man? Coming to beat me with your fists?" And he laughed, echoing in the space of the stairwell. "Look, old man—I could kill you right here, or turn you in. But if you go nice-like and leave Kathy and me be, I'll let you live out your days in peace. And no more peekaboo at the ration center either, deal?" And he smiled a winning smile.

Sam screamed and rushed up the stairs, his body a knotted mass of hate and pain. He clutched at Andrews's throat. The younger man kicked him in the stomach. Sam doubled over and fell on his back.

As Sam tried to get up, Andrews turned and went through the door back into the building. Sam stood up and staggered after him through the swinging door. He stepped into the hall just in time to see Andrews pause in front of the door to his apartment.

"Andrews, listen good!" Sam shouted. "You'll never get rid of me—it's me she wants. There's nothing you can do."

Andrews ignored him. The younger man opened the door

to the apartment and went inside. Sam leaned against the wall in the hallway and tried to catch his breath. In a moment Harry Andrews came out again. There was a gun in his hand.

"I'm taking you down to the nearest police station on a citizen's arrest," Andrews said as he came down the hall toward Sam. "They can check you over at the euthanasia station after I tell them I caught you trying to break into the hospital. You tried to bribe me for some drugs..."

Sam turned and pushed through the door to the stairs and started down quickly. As he turned on the second landing, Andrews shouted after him. "If I shoot you trying to escape, like, it'll be easier—especially after the autopsy shows your sickness!" Sam reached the ground floor and burst out into the dark street. He started running uptown. He looked over his shoulder. Andrews was not there.

Sam knew then that Harry Andrews was playing with him, that he intended to kill him and maybe say nothing to the police or anyone; not even Kathy.

As he ran Sam thought of Kathy. How far away she seemed now, like someone he had known in another life on a different world. If Andrews killed him, Sam Brickner would disappear from Kathy's life and no one would look for him. In an over-crowded city he was not important enough to qualify as a legitimate missing person. A check of his age would be enough for the police to close his file. Even if Andrews let them find his body, and he would not, it would be unprofitable to search for the murderer of a fifty-three-year-old man.

Sam stopped and listened for footsteps behind him. He looked around at the run-down buildings of the old east side. He was near the river; many of these buildings had been condemned a hundred times, and a few blocks ahead had recently been sealed off. The air smelled of brick dust and sewage-polluted river water.

He heard slow footsteps somewhere behind him. A thought pushed into his mind like a cold ice pick. There had to be more to Kathy and Andrews, more than Andrews using him to put a leash on Kathy.

Sam turned a corner and ran toward the river, a suspicion forming in his mind. The footsteps turned into staccato running sounds behind him, echoing out of step with his own.

Suddenly to his right the block ended, turning into a rubble-filled lot and a view of the dark river flowing dead toward an unseen ocean. Sam stepped into the moonlight shadow of the last building and waited. He reached down and picked up a rock. The steps grew louder. In the east the coming dawn was a sickly gray stain of light, and the last quarter moon was a bloated grainy yellow balloon sitting on a rooftop.

The figure came by Sam and stopped with its back to him. Sam hurled the rock at its head and the mannequin crumpled. He did not feel as angry as he thought he would be.

He dragged the still-breathing body into the empty lot near the wall of the building. He sat down next to it, removed the man's gun, and waited.

Harry Andrews coughed and the cough turned into a laugh.

"That's good, old man—but you don't have it to kill me."

Sam pointed the gun at the man's head, saying, "Now tell me what you and Kathy are really up to."

In the faint morning light Sam saw the look of uncertainty in the man's face as he looked at the barrel of his own automatic. Andrews shrugged. "I really do love her too, you know."

"What else?"

"It won't do you any good to know."

"Out with it!"

"Katherine feeds me the regular medication-type drugs, like insulin, for instance. I sell them on the street to those who are hiding things, like you for instance. I set up your doctor's appointment when you needed it, old man." Andrews shrugged again. "Who would have thought Kathy would fall for you? She was mine before, you know, and will be again after I sing about you. I have too much on her. There's a chain of illegal medical practice and medication that runs clear into Canada, and she's plugged into it. You should kill me now, but you won't, you can't." Andrews coughed again, and Sam saw him touching the back of his head. "You bastard," Andrews said, "you've opened my scalp!"

Suddenly Andrews swung at the gun, knocking it from Sam's hand. It clattered in the rubble. Andrews crawled, half leaped onto Sam, reaching for his face. Sam tried to kick and fell backward, the sharp debris pushing into his back. Andrews grasped him tightly around the middle and pulled himself into a sitting position on top of Sam's chest. Then he reached forward and put his hands around Sam's neck. Sam saw him— a dark figure towering against a pale sky. Slowly the hands tightened their grip, until Sam started gasping for breath. A voice said, "I gotta do it, old man—it's the only way. You're two headaches for me. You know too much and I couldn't stand living without her. You too, so it'll be easier on you this way." Sam was climbing a rope of glass winding into a black sky. The rope was suspended over an abyss. The glass crumbled in his hands like sugar, bloodying his palms, and he fell...

Sam thrashed around desperately, trying to get some air into his lungs. His hand closed on a rock and he brought it up and hit Andrews in the temple, caving it in with a crunch. The younger man's grip loosened and he fell on top of Sam.

Sam lay still for a moment, taking in greedy mouthfuls of air. He crawled out from under the corpse embracing him and rested next to it. He thought about Kathy. He had known only a carefully selected portion of her, what she wanted him to see, what he wanted her to be.

The sky grew lighter. Everything seemed so calm now, so peaceful. Maybe he could take Harry's place, if he recovered. Harry had tried to kill him, but he had also helped him live. How many others benefitted? Someone would have to take his place.

Maybe Sam Brickner deserved to die, after all? Maybe he should never see her again, take no more treatments, and let only the strongest survive in a roomier world? That world might have a chance to look outward again to the stars, dream again, and maybe love better than he had. It could all be arranged.

He got up and covered the body with stones. As he worked he realized that he had not known Harry Andrews very well; they had both known only each other's hate and violence. When he was done it was almost fully light. He looked down into a small pool of rainwater in the rubble, wondering how he could ever explain to Kathy how he felt. The face which looked up at him betrayed nothing, a face wrapped in a shadow, a silhouette against a white sky.

Heathen God

". . . every heathen deity has its place in the flow of existence."

THE isolation station and preserve for alien flora and fauna on
Antares IV had only one prisoner, a three-foot-tall gnome-like
biped with skin like creased leather and eyes like great glass
globes. His hair was silky white and reached down to his
shoulders, and he usually went about the great natural park
naked. He lived in a small white cell located in one of the huge
block-like administration modules. There was a small bed in
the cell, and a small doorway which led out of the park. A
hundred feet away from the door there was a small pool, one
of many scattered throughout the park. It reflected the deep-
blue color of the sky.

The gnome was very old, but no one had yet determined
quite how old. And there seemed to be no way to find out.
The gnome himself had never volunteered any information
about his past. In the one hundred years of his imprisonment
he had never asked the caretaker for anything. It was rumored
among the small staff of Earthmen and humanoids that the
gnome was mad. Generally they avoided him. Sometimes they
would watch his small figure gazing at the giant disk of Antares
hanging blood red on the horizon, just above the well-pruned

trees of the park, and they would wonder what he might be thinking.

The majority of Earthpeoples spread over twelve star systems did not even know of the gnome's existence, much less his importance. A few knew, but they were mostly scholarly and political figures, and a few theologians. The most important fact about the alien was that sometime in the remote past he had been responsible for the construction of the solar system and the emergence of intelligent life on Earth.

The secret had been well kept for over a century.

In the one hundred and fourth year of the alien's captivity, two men set out to visit him. The first man's motives were practical: the toppling of an old regime; the other man's goal was to ask questions. The first man's political enemies had helped him to undertake this journey, seeing that it would give them the chance to destroy him. The importance of gaining definitive information about the alien was in itself enough reason to send a mission, but combined with what they knew about the motives of the man they feared, this mission would provide the occasion to resolve both matters at the same time. The second man would bring back anything of value that they might learn about the gnome.

Everything had been planned down to the last detail. The first ship, carrying the two unsuspecting men, was almost ready to come out of hyperspace near Antares. Two hours behind it in the warp was a military vessel—a small troop ship. As the first vessel came out of nothingness into the brilliance of the great star, the commander of the small force ship opened his sealed orders.

As he came down the shuttle ramp with his two companions, Father Louis Chavez tried to prepare himself for what he would find here. It was still difficult to believe what his superiors had told him about the imprisoned alien. The morning air of Antares IV was fresh, and the immediate impression was one of stepping out into a warm botanical garden. At his left Sister Guinivere carried his small attaché case. On his right walked Benedict Compton, linguist, cultural anthropologist, and as everyone took for granted, eventual candidate for first secretary of Earth's Northern Hemisphere. Compton was po-

tentially a religious man, but the kind who always demanded
an advance guarantee before committing himself to anything.
Chavez felt suspicious of him.

On earth the religio-philosophic system was a blend of evolutionary Chardinism and Christianity, an imposing intellectual structure that had been dominant for some two hundred
years now. The political structure based its legitimacy and
continuing policies on it. Compton, from what he had learned,
had frightened some high authorities with the claim that the
gnome creature here on Antares IV was a potential threat to
the beliefs of mankind. This, combined with what was already
known about the alien's past, was seemingly enough to send
this fact-finding mission. Only a few men knew about it, and
Chavez remembered the fear he had sensed in them when he
had been briefed. Their greatest fear was that somehow the
gnome's history would become public knowledge. Compton,
despite his motives, had found a few more political friends.
But Chavez suspected that Compton wanted power not for
himself, but to do something about the quality of life on earth.
He was sure the man was sincere. How little of the thought in
our official faith filters out into actual policy, Chavez thought.
And what would the government do if an unorganized faith—
a heresy in the old sense—were to result from this meeting
between Compton and the alien? Then he remembered how
Compton had rushed this whole visit. He wondered just how
far a man like Compton would go to have his way in the world.

Antares was huge on the horizon, a massive red disk against
a deep blue sky. A slight breeze waved the trees around the
landing square. The pathway, which started at the north corner,
led to three bright white buildings set on a neat lawn and
surrounded by flowering shrubs and fruit-bearing trees. The
walk was pleasant.

Rufus Kade, the caretaker, met them at the front entrance
to the main building. He showed them into the comfortable
reception room. He was a tall, thin botanist, who had taken
the post because it gave him the opportunity to be near exotic
plants. Some of the flora came from worlds as much as one
hundred light-years away from Antares. After the introductions
were over, Kade took the party to the garden where the gnome
spent most of his time.

"Do you ever talk with him, Mr. Kade?" Father Chavez asked. The caretaker shook his head. "No," he said. "And now I hope you will excuse me, I have work to do." He left them at the entrance to the garden path.

Compton turned to Father Chavez and said, "You are lucky, you're the only representative of any church ever to get a chance to meet what might be the central deity of that church." He smiled. "But I feel sorry for you—for whatever he is, he will not be what you expect, and most certainly he will not be what you want him to be."

"Let's wait and see," Chavez said. "I'm not a credulous man."

"You know, Chavez," Compton said in a more serious mood, "they let me come here too easily. What I mean is they took my word for the danger involved with little or no question."

"Should they have not taken your word? You are an important man."

Sister Guinivere led the way into the garden. On either side of them the plants were luxurious, with huge green leaves and strange varicolored flowers. The air was filled with rich scents, and the earth gave the sensation of being very moist and loosely packed. They came into the open area surrounding the pool. Sister Guinivere stood between the two men as they looked at the scene. The water was still, and the disk of Antares was high enough now in the morning sky to be reflected in it.

The gnome stood on the far side, watching them as they approached, as if he expected them at any moment to break into some words of greeting. It would be awkward standing before a member of a race a million years older than mankind and towering over him. It would be aesthetically banal, Chavez thought.

As they came to the other side of the pool Compton said, "Let me start the conversation, Father."

"If you wish," Chavez said. *Why am I afraid, and what does it matter who starts the conversation,* he thought.

Compton walked up to the gnome and sat down cross-legged in front of him. It was a diplomatic gesture. Father Chavez felt relieved and followed the example, motioning Sister Guinivere to do the same. They all looked at the small alien.

His eyes were deep-set and large; his hair was white, thin

and reached down to his shoulders. He had held his hands behind his back when they had approached, but now they were together in front of him. His shoulders were narrow and his arms were thin. He wore a one-piece coverall with short sleeves.

Chavez hoped they would be able to talk to him easily. The gnome looked at each of them in turn. It became obvious that he expected them to start the conversation.

"My name is Benedict Compton," Compton said, "and this is Father Chavez and Sister Guinivere, his secretary. We came here to ask you about your past, because it concerns us."

Slowly the gnome nodded his head, but he did not sit with them. Compton gave Chavez a questioning look.

"Could you tell us who you are?" Chavez asked. The gnome moved his head sharply to look at him. *It's almost as if I interrupted him at something,* Chavez thought. There was a sad look on the face now, as if in that one moment he had understood everything—why they were here and the part he would have to play.

Chavez felt his stomach grow tense. He felt as if he were being carefully examined. Compton was playing with a blade of grass. Sister Guinivere sat with her hands folded in her lap. Briefly he recalled the facts he knew about the alien—facts which only a few Earthmen had been given access to over the last century. Facts which demanded that some sort of official attitude be taken.

The best-kept secret of the past century was the fact that this small creature had initiated the events which led to the emergence of intelligent life on Earth. In the far past he had harnessed his powers of imagination to a vast machine, which had been built for another purpose, and had used it to create much of the life on Earth. He had been caught at his experiments and exiled. Long before men had gone out to the stars he had been a wanderer in the galaxy, but in recent years he had been handed over to Earth authorities to keep at this extraterrestrial preserve. Apparently his people still feared his madness. This was all they had ever revealed to the few Earthmen who took charge of the matter.

It was conjectured that the gnome's race was highly isolationist; the gnome was the only member of it who had ever been seen by Earthmen. The opinion was that his culture feared

contact with other intelligent life, and especially with this il-
legitimate creation. Of the few who knew about the case, one
or two had expressed disbelief. It was after all, Chavez thought,
enough to make any man uneasy. It seemed safer to ignore the
matter most of the time.

Since that one contact with Earth, the gnome's race had
never come back for him. A century ago they had simply left
him in Earth orbit, in a small vessel of undeniably superior
workmanship. A recorded message gave all the information
they had wanted to reveal. Their home world had never been
found, and the gnome had remained silent. Benedict Compton
had set up this meeting, and Chavez had been briefed by his
superiors and instructed to go along as an observer.

Chavez remembered how the information had at first shaken
and then puzzled him. The tension in his stomach grew worse.
He wondered about Compton's motives, but he had not dared
to question them openly. On Earth many scientists prized the
alien as the only contact with a truly advanced culture, and he
knew that more than one young student would do anything to
unlock the secrets that must surely exist in the brain of the
small being now standing in front of him. He felt sure that
Compton was hoping for some such thing.

Suddenly the small figure took a step back from them. A
small breeze waved his long white hair. His small, gnarly body
took on a strange stature; his face was grief-stricken and his
low voice was sad. It wavered as he spoke to them. "I made
you to love each other, and through yourselves, me. I needed
that love. No one can know how much I needed it, but it had
to be freely given, so I had to permit the possibility of it being
withheld. There was no other way, and there still is not."

Chavez looked at Compton. The big man sat very still. Sister
Guinivere was looking down at the grass in front of her feet.
Chavez felt a stirring of fear and panic in his insides. It felt as
if the alien was speaking only to him—as if *he* could relieve
the thirst that lived behind those deep-set eyes in that small
head.

He felt the other's need. He felt the deprivation that was
visible on that face, and he felt that at any moment he would
feel the awesome rage that would spill out onto them. This
then, he thought, is the madness that his race had spoken about.

All the power had been stripped from this being, and now he was a beggar.

Instead of rage there was sadness. It was oppressive. What was Compton trying to uncover here? How could all this benefit anyone? Chavez felt his left hand shaking, and he gripped it with the other hand.

The gnome raised his right hand and spoke again. *Dear God, help me,* Chavez prayed. *Help me to see this clearly.* "I fled from the hive mind which my race was working toward," the gnome said in a louder voice than before. "They have achieved it. They are one entity now. What you see in this dwarfed body are only the essentials of myself—the feelings mostly—they wait for the day when the love in my children comes to fruition and they will unite, thus recreating my former self—which is now in them. Then I will leave my prison and return to them to become the completion of myself. This body will die then. My longing for that time is without limit, and I will make another history like this one and see it through. Each time I will be the completion of a species and its moving spirit. And again they will give birth to me. Without this I am nothing."

There was a loud thunderclap overhead, the unmistakable sound of a shuttle coming through the atmosphere. *But it was too early for the starship shuttle to be coming back for them,* Chavez thought. Compton jumped up and turned to look toward the administration buildings. Chavez noticed that the gnome was looking at him. *Do your people worship a supreme being?* Chavez thought the question. *Do they have the idea of such a being? Surely you know the meaning of such a being?*

I don't know any such thing. The thought was clear in his head. *Do you know him?*

"It's a shuttle craft," Compton said.

Chavez got up. Sister Guinivere struggled to her feet. "What is it?" she asked.

"I—I don't know who it could be," Compton said. Chavez noticed the lack of confidence in the other's voice. Behind them the gnome stood perfectly still, unaffected by the interruption.

"They've landed by now," Compton said. "It could only be one thing, Father—they've found out my plans for the gnome."

Compton spoke in a low voice. "Father, this is the only way to get a change on Earth—yes, it's what you think, a cult, with me as its head, but the cause is just. Join me now, Father!"

Then it's true, Chavez thought. *He's planning to by-pass the lawful candidacy. Then why did they let him come here?*

There was a rustling in the shrubs around the pool area. Suddenly they were surrounded by armed men. Twenty figures in full battle gear had stepped out from the trees and garden shrubs. They stood perfectly still, waiting.

Antares was directly overhead now, a dark-red circle of light covering ten percent of the blue dome that was the sky. Noontime.

Compton's voice shook as he shouted, "What is *this?* Who the devil are you!"

A tall man immediately on the other side of the pool from them appeared to be the commanding officer. He wore no gear and there were no weapons in his hands. Instead he held a small piece of paper which he had just taken out of a sealed envelope.

"Stand away, Father, and you too, Sister!" the officer shouted. "This does not concern you." Then he looked down at the paper in his hand and read: "Benedict Compton, you have been charged with conspiracy to overthrow the government of the Northern Hemisphere on Earth by unlawful means, and you have been tried and convicted by the high court of North America for this crime. The crime involves the use of an alien being as your co-conspirator to initiate a religious controversy through a personally financed campaign which would result in your becoming the leader of a subversive cult, whose aim would be to seize power through a carefully prepared hoax. You and your co-conspirator are both mortal enemies of the state." The officer folded the paper and put it back in its envelope and placed it in his tunic.

Chavez noticed that Sister Guinivere was at his side, and he could tell that she was afraid.

Compton turned to Chavez. "Father, protect the gnome, whatever he is. Use what authority you have. They won't touch you."

"The execution order is signed by Secretary Alcibiad herself!" the tall officer shouted.

Chavez was silent.

"Father, please!" Compton pleaded. "You can't let this happen." Chavez heard the words, but he was numb with surprise. The words had transfixed him as effectively as any spear. He couldn't move, he couldn't think. Sister Guinivere held his arm.

Suddenly Compton was moving toward the gnome.

"Shoot!"

The lasers reached out like tongues.

The little figure fell. And the thought went out from him in one last effort, reaching light-years into space. *I loved you. You did not love me, or each other*. They all heard the thought, and it stopped them momentarily. Compton was still standing, but his right arm was gone, and he was bleeding noisily onto the grass.

"Shoot!"

Again the lasers lashed out. Compton fell on his back, a few yards from the gnome. Sister Guinivere collapsed to her knees, sobbing. She began to wail. The soldiers began to retreat. Father Chavez sat down on the ground. He didn't know what to do. He looked at the two bodies. There was smoke coming from Compton's clothing. The gnome's hair was aflame.

The tall officer now stood alone on the other side of the pool. Chavez knew that his orders had probably been sealed, and he only now felt their full force. After a few moments the tall officer turned and went after his men.

The alien knew this would happen, Chavez thought. *He knew, and that was why he told us everything*.

When the great disk of Antares was forty-five degrees above the horizon, Rufus Kade came out to them. He put the two bodies in plastic specimen bags. Sister Guinivere was calm now and was holding Father Chavez's hand. They both stood up when Kade finished with the bodies.

"They had an official pass from way up," Kade said. "I even checked back on it."

He walked slowly with them to the administration building.

• • •

Father Chavez sat alone in his small cabin looking at the small monitor which showed him where he had been. Soon now the brilliance of the stars would be replaced by the dull emptiness of hyperspace. Antares was a small red disk on the screen.

Momentarily Chavez resented the fact that he had been a mere creation to the gnome. In any case the alien had not been God. His future importance would be no greater than that of Christ—probably less. He had been only an architect, a mere shaper of materials which had existed long before even his great race had come into being. But still—was he not closer to God than any *man* had ever been? Or would be?

The completion for which the gnome had made man would never take place now. The point of mankind's existence as he had made it was gone. And the alien had not known God. If there was such a being, a greatest possible being, he now seemed hopelessly remote...

O Lord, I pray for a sign! Chavez thought.

But he heard only his thoughts and nothing from the being who would surely have answered in a case like this. And he had stood by while they killed the gnome there in the garden by the pool, on that planet circling the red star whose diameter was greater than the orbit of Mars. Despite all his reasoning now, Chavez knew that he had stood back while they killed that part of the small creature which had loved humanity.

But what had he said? The *rest* of the gnome's being *was* humanity, and it still existed; except that now it would never be reunited with him. "Do not fear," the holy Antony had said three thousand years ago, "this goodness as a thing impossible, nor its pursuit as something alien, set a great way off: it hangeth on our own arbitrament. For the sake of the Greek learning men go overseas... but the city of God is everywhere... the kingdom of God is within. The goodness that is in us only asks the human mind." *What we can do for ourselves,* Chavez thought, *that's all that is ours now.*

He took a deep breath as the starship slipped into the nothingness of hyperspace. He felt the burden of the political power which he now carried as a witness to the alien's murder, and he knew that Compton's life had not been for nothing. He would have to hide his intentions carefully, but he knew what he would have to do.

In time, he hoped anew, we may still give birth to the semblance of godhood that lives on in mankind, on that small world which circles a yellow sun.

Interpose

If Christ has not been raised, then our preaching is in vain and your faith is in vain.

—*Corinthians 15:14*

His unwashed clothes were pasted to his lean body with warm sweat. As he moved slowly down the litter-strewn street, he thought of fresh blood running on green wood, refusing to mingle with the last droplets of sap. The noonday sun heated the layer of dust on the sidewalk. A gust of hot wind whirled it into his face. He tried to shield himself with his right hand, but the grit penetrated into his eyes, making them water.

He staggered to the open doorway of a deserted building and sat down on the doorsill. It was cooler here and he was grateful no one had found it before him.

As his eyes cleared, he sat looking at the limbo of the street. A stream of dirty water was flowing in the gutter. A roach ran across the sidewalk in front of him, and a gust of wind swept the insect into the current which carried it away toward the drain on the corner.

The spear entered his side, but only enough to jar him from his shock sleep, enough for him to feel that he was too high on the cross for it to reach his heart. The pain penetrated layers

71

of memory, bridging more than these last twenty years of pavement, to a time before they had marooned him here, and sometimes dimly to a time still earlier. *His eyes were heavy with blood and sweat; his face was benumbed. The wood groaned with his hanging weight. It was green and pliant and the nails were loose in the pulp. The ropes around his arm muscles had shrunk and were biting into his bones.*

The land was dark except for the thin ribbon of dawn on the horizon. Someone was struggling with a ladder on the ground. Soon hands were removing the nails from his palms and cutting the ropes from his arms. He felt himself lowered roughly and wrapped in a cold cloth.

Voices. They were not speaking Aramaic, but he understood them. He heard their thoughts and the words which followed took on meaning. "It couldn't be him, look at his face, not with that face, look at his face."

Another voice echoed, "That face, that face, faceface."

"So many hangermen strung up at this time, impossible to tell for sure, for sure."

"For sure impossible."

"Anyway he was a man like this one. We'll have fun, fun with him as well, just as well."

A third voice shouting, "Hurry, hurry, the machine is swallowing power parked in time." A laugh, a giggle. "Lots of power, gulping and waiting for us—where do we take him after we fix him?"

"Shut up!" A voice with depth, commanding attention from the shallower cortex which mimed him. "See how afraid he is . . ."

Other voices. "See how afraid, afraidafraid!"

"We'll see how afraid he is and take it from there."

"From there, from there, fromthere."

Earlier in the garden he had asked to be taken away from this place where they were planning his death. The saving of men was not a task for him. He had done enough in helping mutate the animals into men, and more in making sure that all the main groups remained isolated long enough to breed true; he had even worked with the others trying to imprint food and hygiene commands on the groups. He would leave it to others to set the examples for the development of a sane culture. The trouble with men seemed to lie in their excessive awe of nature and their own capacities, an impressionability which led them to be convinced only by powers and authorities beyond them, or by the force of the stronger ones among them. Reason was powerless unless allied with one of these. He was not going to die for these creatures, he had decided in the garden, but they had come and seized him while his attention was with communicating . . .

"He'll take some fixing," the dominant voice said. "I wonder if he knows what's happening?"

Another voice was saying, "If it's really him, then he knows. All that brotherly stuff—and from a wreck who crawled away after they cut him down, and all the nothings made up a story. When we cut him up, we'll know for sure." And he laughed.

"Cut him up, cut him up, cuthimup!"

Later he woke up on the floor of a small room. He saw their boots near him. They were looking at the open door where the world was an insubstantial mist, a maelstrom of time flowing by in wave after wave of probability moving outward from a hidden center which somewhere cast the infinite field of space and time and possibility. He felt the bandages on his body and the lack of pain. Time travel, he understood from their thoughts. How cunning and irrational they had become to make it work, a thing so dangerous, absurd and impossible that no race in the galaxy had ever succeeded in making it work. And like the ones who had put him on the cross, they had come for him to soothe their own hatred and cruelty through pain in the name of pleasure. The beast's brain was still served by technical cleverness, so many centuries hence.

Suddenly with a great effort he lifted himself from the floor, and without standing up completely threw himself head first through the open portal, tumbling head over heels into the haze, hearing them screaming behind him as he floated away from the lighted cube. "We'll get you!" they shouted as their light faded and their forms were carried into time . . .

By 1935 he had been alone for twenty years, slowly learning what his disciples had done after his disappearance. Matthew, Mark, Luke and John had lied, creating a fantastic legend. Their written words only served as a reminder of who he really was. The words which he read in the public library remembered everything for him.

But he had not saved mankind, either in terms of the story or his own mission. His death was needed to complete the story, and his presence with the resources of his entire civilization, twenty centuries ago. He had not heard his people's voice in a long time, an age since the time in the garden when the sun had hung in the trees like a blood-red orange.

He took out his small bottle of cheap whiskey and gulped a swallow, grateful for the few lucid moments in which he knew himself, knew he was not the man the apostles and time had made him. The bottle slipped from his grasp and shattered on the pavement. He looked at the pieces, then bent his head and closed his eyes. The reality of his world, so filled with knowledge and the power over one's life, was so distant, and his exile and suffering so near and unfulfilled. Silently he spoke the words which would have freed him in the other time, but were ineffectual here.

He tried to look through shadow to the time before he became a man, and it was a dream filled with light he had lived somewhere, the shards of a madman's memory delivering him into an abyss of doubt. Why should not the recorded version be any more true than his memory of his home world?

He did not know who he was; he could not prove anything to himself, or anyone else. A proof of his divine origin would deny men the choice of following his example. Only fools would fail to bet on a sure thing. His followers had followed him first, then they had been given their proof; mistaken as it was, it had passed for reality. He thought of how many had followed his name during the last twenty centuries, believing in him even when it had meant their deaths.

The others, the men from the future—they had wanted a living creature to play with, to harm in the way that human wreckage was used and dumped from speeding cars in this evil time around him. They had not had their fill with him, at least. But there was no judgement in his mind, only the awareness of the life he could not lead, the powers he could not enjoy, and the knowledge that he would die eventually, never knowing again the perspective of his own kind.

Slowly the sun came lower into the west and hung swollen

over the stone alleys of the city, casting its still warm rays against the face of the building and into the doorway where he was sitting. In front of him the whiskey was dry around the broken glass. An old dog crept by, sniffed at the remains and continued down the street.

His thoughts faded as he tried to remember. It was difficult to remain alert. The sun took an eternity to go down behind the building across the street, but finally it left him in a chill shadow, trying to make sense of the thought of places beyond the world and the bits of conversation floating in his mind.

"Why take the effort? It's like dozens of worlds. They're intelligent, but it's all in the service of the beast."

"Maybe an example might make all the difference—stimulate their rationality through belief. It's worked on many worlds. The sight of a man who was also more than one of them, a man who visibly lives the best in them, maybe it would work here too."

"Whoever took the job would be in for it—the experience would alter him permanently," the first voice said.

"Karo wants to isolate a new group, work on their genetic structure, maybe supplement it with some teaching."

"Karo has always underestimated the power of persuasive forces, and any creature's ability to alter its own choices and tendencies . . ."

He had come among them, taking the place of an unborn man in a human womb; and the mother had come to the cross to cry for her son.

It was so hard to remember. He still found it deadening to think that these creatures from the future had developed time travel, had taken him from the cross and had made it possible for him to have lived so long in this city. The words in the book—maybe they were truer? No one from his own world had ever thought of making time travel a working reality. They would never find him here.

He started to cough as the darkness filled the stone corners of the deserted street, and he felt the sidewalk grow colder under his feet. The evil ones from the future had taken his life, saving it for their own pleasure; his own kind had forsaken him centuries ago.

His mind clouded; it was more than the alcohol. The shock

of appearing in a specific time after he had tumbled out of the shuttle, after he had floated for an eternity in the faintly glowing mists, had left him with sudden discontinuities in his thinking and consciousness, as if his mind were trying to regain the other place, the high ground of his original locus, the place he looked up to now from the bottom of a dark hole.

He heard footsteps in the darkness to his right.

Shapes entered the world, came near him and squatted on the pavement. Suddenly a can of garbage caught fire in the middle of the street and the quick dancing glow showed three ragged figures warming themselves, their shadows jet black crows on the walls of the deserted brick tenements.

One of the men walked over to him and said, "Hey Hal, there's an old guy here in the doorway, come see!"

The other two came over and looked at him. He looked up at them with half closed eyes. He was sure they were not from the future.

"Too bad—he wouldn't be here if he had anything valuable on him."

He tried to sit up straighter on the doorstep, to show them he thought more of himself. Their stares were making a mere *thing* of him, something to be broken. He felt it in them, and the wash of hopelessness in himself.

"We could take his clothes," one said. They were all unshaven and dirty, their elbows showing through their sleeves.

"Why do you wish to harm me?" he asked.

"Listen, old man, you're not going to last long when it gets cold. We can use your clothes."

"Do you have a drink? I dropped mine . . ."

"Okay, let's strip him down. Now."

They came at him, blotting out the light of the fire. Almost gently they began to remove his clothes, moving his arms and legs as if they were the limbs of a mannequin. His body tensed and he became an object in their hands, forgetting where or who he was. Their arms held him like constricting snakes.

He felt a spasm in his right leg and he caught one of them in the crotch with a sudden kick. The man doubled over in pain and fell backward onto the pavement, revealing the fire behind him suddenly.

"Kill him!" he shouted from where he lay. "Kill the bastard!" And he howled from his pain.

The others started to kick him. *"Interpose a god to change animals into men, stir a noble ideal in their beast's brain."* He felt his ribs break, first on one side and then the other, and they hurt as his body rolled on the pavement from their blows. *"We've been fortunate on our world, we have to help where there is even a chance, even a small chance."* The words of his co-workers on the project whispered to him softly, but he could not remember the individuals who had spoken them.

"Take his clothes off," the groaning man said from the pavement where he still lay. "Make it hurt good!"

When he was naked one of them kicked him in the neck, exploding all the pain inside his head. For a brief instant he had a vision of the vandals from the future materializing on the street to carry him away; but he knew that they were the same as these who tormented him now.

Two of them rolled him near the fire and he felt its warmth on his bare skin. "Can you spare me?" he whispered. A hot stone from the fire touched his back, settling into his flesh as if it were plastic. His thoughts fled and the pain was a physical desolation. He did not know who he was; he knew only that he was going to die.

A sense of liberation passed through his being as his body shuddered. He closed his eyes and hung on to the darkness. He felt them grab his feet and drag him closer to the fire. Hot sparks settled on his skin . . .

But he knew now that the lie of his death of long ago would become the truth. He had to die now, violently at their hands to make good all the writings and prophecies—to make worthy the faith which was linked to his name. Only this could release him to return home. Suicide would have been useless, accident would not serve to please the Father.

He knew who he was now. The written words were all true, and his only purpose was to fulfill them. He could trust no other memories. He was the Son of God, and he would have to die to hear his Father's voice again. *"The mission, you're a teacher, a man of science, a bringer of culture, remember?"* Lies! The voices died, the deceiver was beaten.

I am Jesus of Nazareth ... I have to be, or my death is for nothing, he said to himself. A great light filled his mind, illuminating all his images of the world's dark places.

He heard a bottle break somewhere near.

The light destroyed all the false memories which the deceiver had sent to plague him.

He was ready.

They turned him on his back, so the wounds on his back would touch the stone hardness. He did not open his eyes, knowing that in a few seconds the mission would be complete. The broken bottle pierced his chest, entering his heart and spilling blood onto the street and into the cavities of his dying human shell.

The History Machine

> *The statement in this box*
> *is false*

> *The statement in this box*
> *is false* only *if it*
> *is true*

THE history machine is instant history.

But the history machine tells lies. When you look at the screen, everything happens because of everything that comes before it. Every event has a cause, which is as it should be; except that we never experience it quite that way. At any point (a strange word because history is an unbroken flow) history might have been different and the history machine can't show *that*—what it feels like to balance on the edge and not know which way things will go. It's all very clear to hindsight, but the inside of things is opaque. What is the feel from behind the eyes on the faces on the history machine?

79

The moment when things could have been otherwise, the moment of freedom as I feel it from the inside, the underside of reality which is human consciousness, is the only interesting thing about any history. The trembling sense that things are always anybody's ballgame.

I was looking at my history machine (at home naturally) and I kept noticing the editing; and I knew all the while that I could take the copy tape out and edit it all my own way and no one would be able to stop me. Things would still be the result of previous things (I'd see to that), except that it wouldn't be our history anymore.

If anything is our history to begin with. If only one thing is missing from recorded history, it has to be false. And the inside of things is always missing. The perception of the present as it happens is always missing; so nothing is our history to begin with. Maybe the history machine is no damn good for anything.

I dreamed for a moment of another kind of history machine, one which would show me the only real events there are—the timeless motions of atoms and molecules and subatomic particles, the interactions of basic forces, the eternal vibrations which are always the same no matter what happens on the visible macro-level, no matter how individual or free it may seem. I knew I might be able to program the computer to simulate such a display; the real thing would be impossible except in a very indirect sort of way. The computer would take its cues from a recorded body of indirect perceptions of what might be going on, and then it would map the events on to a visual display screen. Any direct perception of events on the subatomic level would result in a distortion of those same events; that is, if true perceptions were possible to begin with. At least the history I was getting was the result of some degree of direct viewing.

I wondered about the observer in history.

Then I went to bed, but the history machine wouldn't let me sleep. Time stands still at night; from midnight to morning is an eternity.

Everything is history.

Absolute truth.

Time begins at dawn.

I already knew everything "historical" I had down on tape, but still I could not shut down and sleep. I got up and went down into the living room and looked at my south wall.

It was covered from floor to ceiling with thousands of history tapes, almost eleven thousand, many of them dating back to when I first began to do history. The north wall was covered with all my private history tapes, the ones of my life since I qualified to own a history machine. I have tried to recover some of my life before that, but the process takes time.

The tapes on the walls. Collage. The elimination of consecutive time. Simultaneous events occurring in the same geometric space. Unroll the tapes and time is born.

The east wall was a blank: the screen, my peep-show into time, expensive to have with the computer and wave scanner and all, and difficult to obtain a professional permit for, but well worth the trouble.

I got out the tape I made the first day I got the history machine. It was the kind of thing which was beginning to interest me now. I dropped the tape into the slot on the console and went and sat down in my form-fitted reclining chair . . .

I was suddenly on the wall, watching the history machine on the wall in the picture on the wall.

To record human history accurately, in its completeness, would take as much time as it took the original events to take place. My conventional human history was reasonably complete, essentially correct. Unless, of course, my selective bias was far off the normal one held by most historians in my time.

Historians, the third class of persons eligible for a license to operate and benefit from the history machine. The first class consists of heads of state; the second class are the police. There are only three eligible classes. Certain persons in the first class keep a check on all permit holders.

Nothing can ever escape the gaze of the history machine; every event leaves its residue of atomic and molecular vibrations and can be retrieved and reconstructed; every stirring of a leaf, the monstrous flappings of strange wings in some forgotten corner of the galaxy, can be represented on the field of the history machine if its eye be turned there. Even the faintest echoes still stir somewhere in the great iron bell of space-time.

Everything is history.

Except the flip side of reality, our thoughts, sensations. The outside we wear like clothing.

I watched myself on the wall. That was a long time ago and it made me feel content not to have lost that moment forever; but then, nothing since that time would ever be lost to me. I remembered my dark bushy eyebrows, now white on my face, but still the same on the monitor. Somewhere the wavelength of that color (they were very black then) would continue to exist, immortally vibrant. The history machine would always give me the outside of things, I would remember the inside . . . I would lose nothing, ever.

Nothing.

My wife came into the room on the wall (she's been dead eight years *now*) and I watched her watching me watch the history machine. She looked good. The darkness of her pubic hair on her naked body drew my eyes, blurring the rest of the picture. Then I was watching myself watch myself copulating with my wife. Was that me on the screen? Or was it me sitting there on the screen watching? Was that me? Looking over my own shoulder to the screen on the screen all I could see of my wife was two legs on either side of myself, and her arms thrashing around on the bed. A two-legged biped with hair between its legs. And another. The color on the history machine has always been very good.

Black and white, I was watching World War II on the wall, but it was far more interesting to watch myself watching myself watch the war on the wall. Of course I could always pull out my *straight* copy of the war, but I always like to get a fresh reaction to my previous reactions. Time is mastered by awareness and sense of connection. Lose that and go mad, break the chain of your self's genesis and perpetuation.

History is all point of view and events, and my own reactions, a shrug here, a laugh there, no movement, a grimace, fascinate me. And the further my motion into time away from that first moment when I watched myself watching WW II the more interesting it would all become . . .

Other things to see, I am the astronomer who turns his gaze into his neighbor's windows when the stars have grown tedious and oppressive with their night grandeur . . .

I closed my eyes and heard the girl's high-pitched screaming, faintly, in the center of my brain, faintly, coming from the center of my head—outward . . .

The mushroom over Nagasaki was beautiful on the screen on the screen on the wall. Those vibrations were still etched sharply into the fabric of eternity and most good history machines could still pick them up well. Deep red washes of color, like light playing on the guts of a disembowelled man, I leaned forward to see how many mushrooms there were in the regression of screens on the wall. Most of my other selves leaned forward, except one. I have always preferred the Nagasaki mushroom to the one at Hiroshima.

There were a few faint faces in the picture, repeated within themselves again and again to the vanishing point. Expressionless faces. I never knew when they would appear, these quirks in the continuum of fluttering reality. I knew a few historians who specialized in them, but they were more like artists than historians.

I have learned to ignore the faces.

The tiny red light in the corner of the north wall, my chronical camera, picked up my day's doings in the living room. The house, of course, is peppered with these little ruby lights, gem eyes which see my life. In the night the computer would edit and store the events and facts of my personal history (which is very much tied up with my public life as an historian), even this moment of watching myself watching WW II. In time this tape would interest me also.

I thought of all the history tapes still to be made of earth-history. They could be filled in like the endless decimal numbers in the archaic Dewey system; an infinity of numbers between numbers, the great mass of human doings. An infinity of shots of a man putting on his pants, an infinity of human couplings; but only one Aristotle, only one Gödel to map the limits of human history.

And natural history?

I thought again of my model of physical history, and I knew that our equipment could never make it an actual viewing. It would always be a simulation, at best; like the simulation of the birth of the universe projected on the inside of a dome.

And the future? Are those historians truthful who say that their minds move about in time as bodies of ordinary men move about in space? Does the future cast its emotional shadow backward to us?

In time I knew every tape in my personal history would interest me. They are the cups filled with my existence, precious if I am ever to call my life my own. But always "I"—the plastic, indeterminate project "I"—would flee before my scrutiny, and grasp myself anew with each new recording. I dreamed of a non-relational tape, an absolute record of the past, present and future which would capture all of me and make an end to history and process, and end the watching of my waking self.

The positive print of time would be reversed and I would slip between the folds of reality, fall through the bottom of all surfaces . . . out . . . into where?

Impossible.

Absolute truth.

Everything is history.

I must always watch. My history is complete at the moment of my death, what could have been otherwise in a thousand ways becomes set, closed, motionless, determined, spaceless; my spine dissolves, my atoms drift apart and nothing is left. But history is never complete. My death becomes a historical fact.

There is an event which can never be grasped, because there is always one more event to be added, the fleeing present frame of the observer. "He"—the plastic "I"—can never get outside the observer's awareness, only into another, and still another, like a Chinese box that has no final box within a box.

There is no time before time, no time after time. There is time before this and time after.

Only time.

Everything is history.

I watched the beginnings of WW III, the blossomings of fiery balloons in the Middle-Eastern desert: one after one after one after one after one into the vanishing point. And ghostly expressionless faces from nowhere. I watched myself watching myself watch what I was watching on the screen in the room on the wall where I sat watching the screen on the wall in the house on the screen in the screen where I watched WW III begin.

Reality is a machine within a machine within a machine.

Independent viewing is impossible.

The faces were laughing.

Infinite regress: a form of irrationality, a strong objection to the validity of a line of reasoning. Usually used to dismiss as nonsense any assertion or class of assertions which lead to an infinite regress.

The Cliometricon

This universe is constantly splitting into a stupendous number of branches, all resulting from the measurementlike interactions between its myriad components. Moreover, every quantum transition taking place on every star, in every galaxy, in every remote corner of the universe is splitting our local world on earth into myriads of copies of itself.

—*Bryce S. DeWitt,* "Quantum Mechanics and Reality," *Physics Today, Sept. 1970*

THE cliometricon visualizes alternate histories.

A standard history machine enables us to see history in terms of cause and effect. The cliometricon shows lines of might-have-beens as causal probabilities. Both types of apparatus are inaccurate to the degree that each leaves out the experience-of-events. This phenomenon must be supplied by the trained imaginations of licensed historical observers.

Slowly, subtly, the cliometricon draws the basic quantum transitional processes of time into itself, calculating probabilities (a more general form of causality) more like a banker than a gambler; and we see the stuff of time take $100^{100} + N$ differing directions in the guise of matter and living flesh.

It teaches the class of historians who have been previously restricted to standard home-line history machines a sense of expanded contingency and complex determination. Clio, the muse of history, is wooed with measure and analysis far beyond the linear perceptions of normal observers. Alternate world-lines, we learn, are not mere probabilities in a bloodless realm, but realities in the finer structures of reality.

I am watching General Eisenhower as he walks along the white cliffs of Dover. It is raining and his face is hidden in the shadow under his cap. His eyes move his head to peer across the channel at the dark continent of Europa which seems now forever lost to the will of the failed invasion...

In his mind rise up fearful bloody shadows of men retreating, thrown dying into the sea by Rommel's defenses; whole divisions destroyed, burned and blinded by the relatively mild effects of tactical nuclear artillery. Lost, an entire world of towns and villages and cities, bordered in the east by a giant who will not rise again after being blackened into ash by the full-scale strategic fury of Hitler's thermonuclear whirlwinds. The giant who had been counted on to bleed the most is dead.

I push the clear tab for the If-Continuum System Interlock. Before me, in blue light, appears a figure like myself sitting before a machine with his back to me. On his screen appears another figure; and on his still another; and another, into the vanishing point. System Interlock mode functions check the world lines for integrity. A breakage would show itself as a chaos frame filled with furious noise and random images.

Reality is a matrix of relatively fixed world-lines. If-points exist as potentials in each line. If-points extend themselves from a potentially contingent moment, though not from all such moments, and also become relatively fixed world-lines. It is the overlay of an infinite number of if-lines which produces the perceived experience of contingency, or choice, in an observer. The psychological reality of observers integrates if-lines.

Historians debate whether world-lines are diverging in absolute or relative space, or if they are converging to form an integrated statistically determined world-line. Breakages might be indications of unsuccessful integration processes brought about by unusually fluid thought processes of observers in different lines. As long ago as the 1970's Eugene Wigner had advocated a gross nonlinear departure from Schrödinger's normal equations, indicating what must happen when conscious observers are taken into account. Wigner even proposed that a search be conducted for possible effects of consciousness on matter. Today only a comprehensive System Interlock meeting of scholars might resolve this problem, and perhaps even help in the creation of an integrated line. But this does not seem likely, as not all lines have developed cliometric technology . . .

Cliometrics is a tool of empirical research and record keeping—a significant improvement over the old impressionistic, non-dimensional, often uni-valent written texts. Written texts were always observer distortions, utterances rife with psychological reference errors; reference was made as much to the observer as to the vague historical *object*. The result was a directional product of the two, as well as an historical object of its own time. Experience and subjectivity (both important facts about observers) were conveyed only indirectly. The imaginative memory of so-called novelists was the closest thing to the direct scrutiny of today's licensed temporal observers.

Cliometric technology recreates with precision directly from quantum physical sources, catching through physical implication the play of permutations on the experienced level . . .

There is a wind at Thermopylae.

The Spartan defensive force has not arrived. The moment of might-have-been has passed. The initial *necessary* conditions were present, but the *sufficient* circumstances are absent.

The first Persian scouts are coming through the pass, shielding their faces against the wind . . .

Five thousand Spartans will not lie dead on the rocky ground. Many will never see battle, siring hundreds of children instead. Greece will not be stirred by the death of Leonidas. He will die at the hands of a jealous husband.

As I watch, the efficient cause of all these things comes into view—furies casting shadows onto the stone strewn landscape.

There are wings over Thermopylae, white wings in a sun-windy afternoon. War gliders from Athens. Created by Themistocles's physicists.

As the Persians stream into the pass from their ships on the shore, the Greeks glide in low and drop fireballs on the advancing horde. And when finally Apollo's naphtha runs dry, the gliders turn wings and disappear.

A second squadron appears, riding into the up-drafts from the pass, rocking high above the reach of Persian arrows and lances . . .

Eisenhower pauses at the chalk cliff's edge. He is a dark solid three dimensional shadow in the light, a mere uniform stuffed with unseen flesh.

The screen lights up with an atomic flash, and I know that his flesh is disintegrating, his skeleton is melting. The fortress of England is crumbling. Shakespeare's original folios are ash upon the withering green. I turn down the light streaming from the screen.

Somewhere above, I imagine clearly, the pilotless bomber makes a slow turn and heads back toward the Luftwaffe field in France, where they already know what the bright western dawn means.

Rudolf Hess gets up from the remote control screen. An aide takes over while he goes to the bunker slits to peer out. The returning bomber is a dark insect against the bright orange cumulous of megadeath.

Eisenhower tumbles off the cliff, his torso pierced clean through by a bullet fired leisurely from the deck of the submarine which only a moment ago surfaced offshore and is already beginning to dive.

In the periscope, Eisenhower's falling body looks for just a moment like a black spider floating down on a piece of web. The sea swallows his corpse as his aides look on. From a distance their faces are only patches of white.

The spitfire aircraft will be too late to sink the sub.

We are the heirs of the old cliometricians, who in the twentieth century first married the muse of history to quantification.

No one mind could see meaning in masses of data so huge that light years of distance would be required simply to lay all the bits end to end.

But still the data was finite. It could be enumerated, and even interpreted with the help of our children, the computer minds.

Our task became harder, nevertheless.

The quantum of historical action is multifarious.

Probabilities are infinite. The store of alternatives is eternal, inexhaustible. Only this fact and endless individual events are absolute.

The practice of our profession is safely incomplete. The whole is divinely indefinable and mysterious.

Eisenhower swims to shore. Blood streams from his shoulder and mingles with the sea foam as he struggles onto a rock, where he manages to contain the flow until a boat arrives.

He watches as the submarine is sunk by spitfires.

The cliometricon is an endlessly growing library of visual records (the visual form grew out of the entertainingly contemplative motion picture arts of the twentieth century). Parastatics, the technology of sub-molar engineering, led to the storage of infinite amounts of information within the infinitesimal folds of space-time below the Fermi threshold. Each record is filed with a library of assessments and statistical evaluations. Every observer bias is included and taken into account by the next observer. Naturally, the home-line receives special attention in terms of recorded bulk.

In that moment when he contemplates his plans for the conduct of the war, Eisenhower is joined to the ultimate enigma of time's flow—the forward direction toward a still formless future.

On the screen it appears as a shapeless chaos of the thing-in-itself, the substratum of all that is large and small, the malleable reality of infinite variation. This is, of course, only a visualization, unlike the real-time recovery of overlaid events, which are also considerably more regular.

In Eisenhower's mind it becomes a determination of decision, qualified by the probabilities of physical control during execution: he sees an invasion in which the landing is never made; all ships are sunk or turned back long before the landing barges can be launched; the army comes ashore but is driven back into the sea by an overwhelming panzer force; the allies sweep across Europe, only to be swept back by the Russian army whose commanders still remember Western intervention in their post revolutionary civil war (Dunkirk repeats itself on a larger scale); the allies use nuclear weapons to level Germany, and later all of western Russia...

Between all these events, I can see an infinity of trivial variations and minor crises; while alongside these events lie radical alternatives and their variations.

The continuum of probabilities is infinitely crowded.

World lines growing out of the past thrust insistently into a shapeless future. There is rest in the visualized presence of the formless chaos on the screen. Here I cannot retreat to a point where orderly patterns become visible—the point at which waves seem to be well concentrated around their average length and the quantum of action is negligible, the point in Schrödinger's equations where the shortness of wave lengths permits the classical world of Newton to come into being. Here lies the ultimate irrational. Here the agony of events has no meaning, except that I visualize them.

Individuals perish, but the eyes of intelligence endure, receiving the information which makes a universe exist, ending the chain of infinite regression and possibility of the indeterminate. Without eyes the thing-in-itself is cold and lightless—despite its energy—and alone. The waves of confusion and possibility do not coalesce into solid matter; touch and sight cannot be born.

The consciousness of observers creates time and history. Objectivity is relative, but no less real.

Eisenhower shivers at Dover. Turning away from the sea, he walks up the path to his jeep. He cannot be sure of his world. He can plan, decide and carry out while hovering at the abyss of uncertainty, an edge more fearful than any cliff. In the firmament of time, his character will play all possible roles, an endless fresco painted by the muses of biology and physics. Armies will struggle, are struggling, as I watch him drive away . . .

I push the *minor* System Interlock and watch myself watching him drive away, toward where the road runs close to the edge over the gentle breakers below . . .

The road gives way. I cannot see the effect of Eisenhower's trivial death on my face, unless I turn around and watch my copy do the same in the mirror which I have set up illegally behind myself. I turn around, knowing that I am violating the personal peeping prohibitions. But this is the first time, and perhaps the corps of watchers will not notice.

I want to feel what my alternates feel, at least one. I want to feel his face in mine. I want to know at least one other of the army of observers which fills up the abyss within me. After all, they are all within me, and I live in them. I will risk my tenure and the practice of history-as-usual for this.

A face appears—my own, but much older.

"What do you want? A prolonged link is a violation."

"I want to talk to you."

"There is no time!"

I panic and push the button for a resumption of normal flow.

The universe moves with sleight-of-hand, the unknown becoming known, time unfolding, ignorance leading to discovery and knowledge. I feel the anguish of space-time in a night land chilled by endless icy stars. Time and I unwind from darkness like a glittering snake. Time is the dark pulsing body of the serpent, and I the glitter. Psycho-physical parallelism is the central fact of history . . .

Oppenheimer, Teller and Eisenhower visit the ruins of Moscow, now levelled by strategic nuclear weapons of only low yield, while a world away Speer seeks to recruit Einstein and Bohr for work in the victorious Reich. Teller and Oppenheimer have committed suicide . . .

• • •

Leonidas lies dying in the pass at Thermopylae.

Possibilities are slowly fading from his face, along with the late afternoon sunlight. The soldiers around him look like hard-shelled beetles in their armor. His face is my face, his thoughts my own as death steals over him . . .

There are some who deny the possibility of deducing macro-events from micro-quantum events. The heresy states that what we see on the screens of the cliometricon are imaginative extrapolations based on the wealth of facts and assumptions inherited from the past. Bryce S. DeWitt, a professor of the twentieth century, had recorded that "The quantum realm must be viewed as a kind of ghostly world whose symbols, such as the wave function, represent potentiality rather than reality." If-lines are not real.

Yet . . .

. . . Leonidas *thinks* as he lies dying, and his thoughts press into me. Time passes, he whispers, and I feel vague changes inside, wondering what is this *effort* of time passing, this changing which seems not to change, this journeying near the shore with no goal in sight? Familiarity has dulled the questing in me, hiding enigmas in the robes of everyday, preventing unmapped thoughts. Does time pass where there are no heartbeats? If I could only hold myself perfectly still, stay the mortal blood passing from me into the earth, then I would hear time pass near while never touching me. It would continue to write in the ephemeris of the ephemeral, changing the shape and shadow of all living things, excepting me . . .

An atomic flash, followed by a xenomorphic mushroom.

Oppenheimer says, "I am become death, the shatterer of worlds."

Endless worlds, or the ghosts of chance?

This heresy has the power to consume me.

Stance of Splendor

THEY were two swimmers suspended in a perfectly clear sea, she moving on her back below him, limbs open freely, floating gently; he a perfectly muscled body, sinewy fibers wrapped around bone in a strong grip.

He pushed down to her, grasped her head with both hands, and kissed her.

He saw himself with her, saw the small rings of water moving away from the intertwined bodies. The field of water was filled with light.

He held the water filled globe in his hand, looking at it against the sheet of white light which was the sky, watching the figures turn slowly in the liquid, remembering.

"As I grew up," he told her, "I became afraid that I would be nothing, absolutely nobody. It was a terrible suspicion to have to live with."

"You'll get over it," she said and pulled his head down to hers.

"Look, I don't want to talk about it. I've heard it all before. Enjoy it." He kissed her reluctantly.

The machine gun stitched across the bodies on the ground. He watched grasping hands thrust forward from torsos. His own mouth was in the dirt and he felt the bullet rivet him to the earth.

She came to see him and he felt her eyes looking through the sheets. No arms, no legs. He was nothing.

Drown, sink down, rush out as light into the sea mud, surface into a fog of pain, space filled with white light.

Blink.

His eyes refused to roll down from inside his head. He groped with dead, phantom limbs into the white space, trying to picture something dark and tangible to calm his fear of blindness. His eyes were made of polished marble set in the liquid of his head; nerves brushed gently against their stone surface, nerves of rigid ivory wire trying to pick up something to send backstage.

Blink.

He sensed the surface he was lying on. He pictured stucco set in squares. He tried to sit up, and could not. Inability became a dense, fearful mass in his stomach.

Blink. He closed his eyelids. The white light became a field of dull red covered with capillaries. Fear became a spreading glow reknitting the strands of his consciousness. He felt the raw, cut-off ends of his nerves trying to extend themselves into the absent flesh.

They had said, "We're going to reinforce the matrix of your individuality, the craggy-lightning pattern of your nervous system buried in your flesh, the neural connections of your brain and spine, until the whole is charged enough to stand by itself..."

Without flesh. They had shown him a three dimensional holoimage of a nervous system and brain pattern standing in a display tank—an infinitely delicate skeleton traced in white light, standing naked, fleshless, boneless, a pattern of energy looped back on itself.

Life after death. Immortality.

A man dies and becomes like a ruined house. The beams fall in, the insides rot, and the walls let in light and wind. The intensely alive man, they had said, one of upward spiraling, extreme lifelong consciousness, reaches a point when his brain and nervous system are strong enough to do without the generating engine of the body to sustain the epiphenomenal field of personality and awareness. His life must then become a rush toward greater and more complex awareness, until he is transfigured into a self-sustaining being. They had compared the emergence of trans-man with that moment when sub-man had first groped after consciousness, and had become man.

We are going to do this in a lab, they had said.

He had wondered of the dissolute men, who believe little and reason scarce at all. They get nothing when their bodies dissolve, taking the partially formed permanence of their mind and nervous system with them into the dark.

Then he had passed through the laboratory floor, through the asbestos and tile and foundation and granite rock into the magma-warmth inside the earth, where the heat nourished him. Perception became direct, lacking the distortion of perceiver and object, the imperfection of sense and interpretation which sees the cosmos through the wrong end of time as some shadow play on a basement wall.

The sun's radiance streamed through the earth, a standing gravito-magnetic wave front.

He shrugged, shifting the earth's crust around him, and he knew that he had filled up the earth with himself. How would she understand him now, he thought, how could she continue to love him? He had hung ghostly near the physical tracings, the scratches in time-space and matter which had been his body in the apparatus; and they had not been able to see him to know they had succeeded.

His body had thrashed about, empty eyes open.

"*Hopelessly mad.*" Their uncomprehending masks spoke the words.

A thin whisper of atmosphere at his outer edge: weather. He felt the tidal bulge rush closely along the ocean bottom, slowly shaping it . . . passing.

Pulse. Blink.

It became colder as he drained the planet of energy and was left with the light and tide of the sun, moon and stars to feed him.

Blink. He pulsed the field of the earth as it grew colder, moved the planet with a shrug, wrinkled its skin with a whisper of his will—

—and rolled it into the sun like a ball down a smooth incline, blinking its field on and off, in a long curve which took him into the center, shedding the earth long before he reached it. He filled the sun and it did not drain...

She was gone now too; and there were no others like him anywhere near. Had he ever been something else?

He remembered living in a smaller, dream world, living half awake—

Spinningspinningspinning stop the earth turningturning stop.

Dead stop—millions hurled thousands of miles across the continents. Standing structures knocked flat, pressed down by a giant hand; the air seething with storm clouds and light. And the sun had received the shards...

He breathed in the burning solar gales.

The sun flickered—

—cut off for a second eons of solar streaming into the dark abyss. In a moment the star would not be enough.

He drew himself into a concentrated mass, shaping himself into—

A leaping shout of energy and light, a huge spark jumping between the stars, leaving the sun to collapse into a dark, pitiable thing glowing on the edge of red and black. Dying.

Sirius.

Time was zero, though lesser vantages would have felt the time it had taken. He bathed in the star, his analogical consciousness assuming its form, assimilating its rhythms and profound structure of energy exchange, his accelerated intelligence reaching out to notice the material in orbit around the primary.

There was no one like him...

For a moment the ground was joined to the livid green sky by a two-pronged, misshapen finger of light. In the brief silence the sky became dark again and the moon cast its indifferent white light through a break in the clouds and was swiftly hidden by the woolly masses, the shoulders of protean night travelers moving toward dawn. The sun crouched below the world, held back by the storm. The rain started as a whisper and fell in a rush of crystalline droplets which still held the light of moon and stars in their structures. The thick, rich earth inhaled the flood and worms came to the surface and were washed pink.

The hammer blow struck stone, a god bringing chaos with his presence...

Sirius dimmed, waking him. The light flowing out faltered, leaving the ends to rush away like a tide going out hurriedly.

He reached out to Tau Ceti *Oh God, release me,* he prayed leaving the burned out star. There he drew the binary companion into the main furnace *Make me small as I was before, give back all the lives,* feeding on the massed power. Briefly, the star flared, gobbling up its children *Let me die.*

I deny you! Whatever you are let me go The center of stars, the galactic hearth drew him now. He went whispering between the stars, strong enough to feed on the tenuous gas and radiation between the suns, breathing the galaxy's atmosphere. He went like a beggar toward the locus of endless power, a beggar knocking over garbage cans, devouring the meager scraps and smallest sparks of life *They're all dying, the smallest ant. This lumbering beast was pressing in from all sides, rushing into him with winds and currents and screams, outraged by his small remains, remaking the rest into itself. Anything, help me save me kill me . . . mother!*

Were there others? Or were they simply being silent, fearing the meeting that could only result in one new birth? He hurried, compressing the forces inside himself to crush all remains of the other time, reaching out to the brightest stars, a thousand beacons hanging in the abyss, and made them into himself *He was rushing upward through the floors of a huge iron building made of rusty girders, floors of rotting wood, trap doors open before his rush, dissolving . . .*

The pattern of himself grasped a hundred stars more in its net. His frontier flashed outward . . .

A lifeless body thrashing on the table . . .

His perimeter came to the edge of the galaxy and stopped—

The wheel of stars with its film of gas became his skin, and he filled it up.

The galaxy breathed. Its forces became his pulse.

He hurried, knowing that he was not yet everything.

A huge mass came down and crushed him forever.

And distant fears came close to him, tears moving slowly, leaving acid tracks in his cells as he blotted out his old self, forgetting . . .

He looked out into the dark—

—saw the small lights beyond—

—felt the cold which he could not pass across. He was forced to see in the old way, knowing things different from him, all around him.

He tried to expand at the sight of the infinite emptiness, tried to reach out to those faint brushes of light, almost disintegrated in a huge sigh of stars and gases, and recovered, rested in a state of exaltation...

He began to throb. The island of stars began to pulse faster and faster, pushing against space. He pulled the two companion clouds into his center, flaring the globular clusters around the central vortex across the whole spectrum of light—

—Pulse.

The maelstrom of himself began to suck in dust and radiation into the center of the spiral and spew it out into his arms, spinning the starstorm faster, moving it in a new direction, streaming suns in its wake.

In a moment of eternity he was moving in a monstrous rush toward his new prey, and his light shifted into a dark red...

A fist thrust into the sky, his grasping fingers broke through the cardboard—

—Into a bare room. With white walls and perfect corners.

Wayside World

The city sat in the hill, rising upward from deep within the mass of earth, rock and vegetation to tower a kilometer into the night sky, its angled windows dark, reflecting only the bright stars and the faint rainbow of the ring; ten thousand windows, centuries old and unbroken, staring westward across the valley. Meteors flashed in the plastic panes, mute fireworks showing in black, sightless eyes long past celebration. The structure was an empty shell which had once housed a million people. A few still used it because the windows caught the sunlight, warming the outer layer of dwelling spaces through trapped heat.

At the edge of the world a morning storm flickered in the clouds which hid the dawnlight. The city's clear panels became blinking eyes, the sudden brightness of lightning destroying the mirrored ebony surfaces which held the cold starlight and dying meteor trails.

In rooms a third of the way up from the vegetation of the hillside, six people slept, derelicts in need of a dawn to stir them from their troubled sleep . . .

I

HE opened his eyes suddenly and saw the light flashing through the windows, flooding the world with a blue-white wash. In a moment the drops were beating against the windows, running like tears down the inclines. The rain would make things grow; summer would last just a little longer. Sadness welled up within him. He started to repeat his name in the way his mother had once spoken it.

Call him Ishbok, his father had said a long time ago, but his mother had made it sound special. *Ishbok,* he whispered softly to himself, trying to catch the musical quality of his mother's voice.

The others did not waken, and the storm seemed to rage over their stillness. The water washed downward in a river; the thunder walked with the footsteps of a giant. The full force of the storm rode over the valley, holding back the light of sunrise.

Ishbok looked around at his sleeping companions, at Foler, who also wanted Anneka; at Foler's younger brother, Thessan, who would never be well; at Anneka sleeping next to her dying parents. The old couple were fading fast, sleeping away most of each day; there was nothing to be done except make them comfortable and bring them what little food they were able to eat. *Why could we not have been trees,* Ishbok thought, *or the stones which seem able to keep their pride. We are soft and filled with blood, and a dried sarissa bamboo point is enough to kill us ...*

Foler already spoke as if Anneka belonged to him. His every glance was a challenge. Ishbok was avoiding a fight, hoping that Anneka would say how she felt. Sometimes he felt shamed and angry at her silence. He did not want to fight Foler, even if a fair fight were possible; Thessan would join in like a stupid dog defending his master. The dark-haired older brother's friendly smile hid the truth—he was always ready to let things happen, as long as they served his wants.

After Anneka's mother and father died, Foler would take the daughter. If Ishbok tried to stop it, he would die; if he did nothing, he would live. It was as simple as that. *He's afraid to take her while the old live,* Ishbok thought. *He's afraid of their curses. He fears unseen things more than me. He controls Thessan with his own fears . . .*

For a moment Ishbok imagined what it would be like to be Thessan. Without Foler, nothing was certain. Foler knew where all the food was to be hunted or found; he kept evil things away at night. Foler had to be obeyed; there was no other way. Foler made him feel good; Foler made him feel safe.

Thessan was like a faber, except fabers were much more alert; fabers had pride. Ishbok felt sorry for Thessan; but being sorry would not help him, as hatred would not make his brother better.

Across the room Foler stirred and sat up while prodding Thessan awake. His eyes were watchful, suspicious; but in a moment his gaze became uncaring as he realized that Ishbok would not have waited for wakefulness to kill him. Slowly Foler got to his feet. *He knows I couldn't do it, he's sure of it.*

"Coward!" Foler threw the word like a stone.

Anneka woke up, pulling the blanket around her for protection. She sat up and looked at Ishbok. He thought he saw reproach in her expression, but the light was too faint to be sure. There would be no smile or look of sympathy, only the look of resignation. *Anneka . . . Anneka,* he said silently, *I made none of this, but I love you.*

"Unwind your stringy muscles," Foler said to him, "we have food to find."

The thunder exploded again and water ran in noisy rivulets on the windows. Foler's face was a grinning skull with caves for eyes.

Anneka began to braid her long brown hair, her eyes cast downward. She looked up only to glance at the storm outside.

Ishbok watched her from where he sat on his blanket. His stomach was cold and empty. He shivered, longing for the warm sun and hoping the storm would pass soon; it would make food-searching a little easier.

Anneka's father woke up, breathing badly and coughing.

"The old fool should be dead," Foler said stretching. Then he held out a hand and helped Thessan stand up.

Anneka's mother woke up, wailing about her blindness.

"Keep her quiet," Foler said. Ishbok saw a fearful look take hold of Foler's face. "They should both be dead."

"They'll die, they'll die," Thessan chanted, hoping to please his brother. Foler grinned and patted him on the back.

Suddenly Thessan lumbered across the large room to a window and placed his large palms against the moisture-laden interior surface. He washed his face, chuckling to himself.

"It's a dark rainy morning," Anneka said to her mother, stroking her forehead. Her husband reached over and held her bony hand. The old woman cleared her throat.

Foler went over to the window and slapped some moisture on his face. Ishbok stumbled to his feet and walked over to a fresh window. He cupped some wetness and put it to his face.

Foler laughed. "Not much hair to wash on him."

Ishbok looked up to see Thessan standing next to him, grinning and running his fingers through his dirty beard.

Ishbok turned away from him and took a few steps toward the door.

Anneka tied her braids off with two bits of leather and stood up. "I'm ready," she said.

Foler went past Ishbok and turned in the door. "A strong woman—not for you. With that soft hide of yours, you'd bleed to death from her scratches."

Ishbok felt the anger swell in himself, but he looked away from Foler's eyes.

"You're not worth killing," Foler continued. "One day you'll break your own neck and save me the trouble. You're good for picking roots, berries and nuts. Even Anneka can kill an animal for food." He paused. "Ah, let's get going!" He turned and went out into the hall and toward the stairs. Ishbok followed, thinking suddenly that he might run up behind Foler and push him to his death; but in the next moment he was flat on his face as Thessan pulled his feet out from behind. Ishbok's jaw hurt from the impact. Thessan stumbled across him and ran after his brother, laughing.

Anneka helped him to his feet and walked toward the stairs without a word. Slowly Ishbok followed, feeling no hatred now, only shame and sadness, the coldness in his stomach a heavy weight slowing his steps.

• • •

Foler led them upstream through the center of the valley. Thessan followed close behind him. Anneka walked a dozen paces behind Thessan. Ishbok was last.

The clouds of morning passed. Anneka's hair turned a bright red in the sun rising at their back. Ishbok walked slowly, watching her. Despite her clothing from the oldtime, the patched trousers, leather belt, sweater and boots, she seemed gentle marching across the mossy turf next to the stream.

Morning mists rose from the valley as the sun warmed the earth. The silence of his own breathing and the steadiness of the stream at his right calmed him. Far ahead to his left the red-coned evergreens sat on the mountainside; around them nestled sugarroot bushes, their leaves and pulpy twigs laden with the sweetness of late summer.

Slowly Foler was making a circle which would lead them up into the hills. They would eat the sugarroot, and then there would be enough strength to bring down some game and carry it home. Ishbok licked his lips at the thought of the sugarroot.

Maybe today they would bring down a hipposaur when it came to drink the stream water and graze on the green moss; maybe today luck would give them enough food for a week's rest in the city.

But quickly he remembered that full stomachs and rested muscles would help them forget the need they all had of one another. Foler would want Anneka again; Thessan would be bored and hard to control.

A jumpingtom raced across Foler's path. Foler raised his boomerang and let fly, cursing as it missed. He went to get it back. Ishbok heard more cursing.

"Ishbok, come here!" Foler shouted.

Ishbok hurried.

"It broke on the stone—you'll have to make a new one. Better make two." Foler was almost friendly.

If I make too many spares, Ishbok thought, *you won't need me.* "I can only work so fast," he said softly, "and not at all when I'm hungry and afraid."

Foler's dark eyes were scornful. His eyebrows went up and he grinned through his beard. "I'm the best thrower."

Foler turned away and continued on the path to the sugar-roots. Ishbok followed. Thessan came up behind him and pushed him out of the way to get back near his brother. Ishbok turned his head to see Anneka walking steadily behind him. She did not look up and he turned away to fix his gaze on the red cones ahead.

As he walked he thought of the stories about the old sicknesses, the war plagues, the fireballs that left heaps of dead, the skeletons in the cities. He had never seen any of these things, but his mother's vivid tellings lived in his mind. He remembered his father's look of reproach when he would find her giving such life to the past.

Those who lived had found each other among the dead, in cities which stood unharmed, yet were gutted. The survivors knew the value of human life, acting out of necessity, clinging to each other in resignation and acceptance. So it had been for more than two generations. Ishbok's father and mother had met in the great empty city by the northern lake. From there they had travelled down to the southern ocean, in time for Ishbok to be born in a small stone house near the water. His father had complained that there were few old-time libraries in the smaller southern cities, and that Ishbok would not survive as well in a colder climate as if he were born in a warmer place.

But life will be easier here, his mother had said, *and we don't have to go back.*

He'll have to go back to learn, his father had answered.

When he is older, he'll go back well enough . . .

One day dark men had come out of the swamp to spear his father to a gnarly dwarf tree and carry his mother away like a four-footed animal hanging from a stick, her long black hair dragging on the ground . . .

Ishbok remembered the sick feeling in his stomach as he had been picked up and hurled down from a cliff into the sea. But his small body had missed the rocks. His cheek touched bottom gently and he pushed himself upward with his hands. He swam as he had been taught and the waves washed him ashore with only a few cuts from the rocks. He remembered his own blood on the sand when he had gotten up hours later, his tears burned away by the hot sun.

The little house was empty when he returned. In the silence of sea and memory he heard again his father's wish that he should learn about the world before life came to an end. When he looked at the body pinned to the tree, he imagined that his father's life had become joined to the twisted trunk, his flesh drinking now the moisture brought up by the tree's deeply searching roots.

Traveling north, he had searched for the libraries which held the books he knew how to read. He could not read all the languages brought to his world, Cleopatra, by the colonists from Earth, but he could always understand his own, and much of two others. The libraries spoke about one another, sending him amongst themselves as would jealous guardians who share a favorite child. The old buildings gave him shelter and knowledge—the knowledge of stored foods and where to find them. In winter the food enabled him to stay in one place as he studied. Once he had been forced to burn a few of the books he could not read to keep warm, telling himself that he would never find anyone who could tell him what they were about. Besides, the books spoke of other kinds of books, known things stored in machines which gave knowledge for the asking; he was sure there was more than one copy of the volumes he had burned.

In the empty cities he had come upon small bands of men and women. Sometimes they would accept him, with suspicion; he would stay for a time, to leave or to be driven off sooner or later.

He had come into Anneka's group five summers ago. Her parents could still walk then. Foler and Thessan had been friendly, especially after finding out he could make knives, spear points and boomerangs—and keep the weapons sharper than they had ever known. But no matter how long Foler watched him work the old metal on the stream stones, he could not match Ishbok's skill. One day Thessan had tried sharpening to please his brother. Foler had beaten him for ruining two knives, but Ishbok had saved the edges.

So little of what he had learned in the libraries could be turned into useful things. Knowledge had made him feel pity, and the need for another kind of learning, barely glimpsed, one which might again create the realities of the old time.

Ishbok turned to look back at the city, set like a blue gem in the mossy mountain, entranceways hidden in foliage. The towering place was always a reminder of exile from a better past. The structure soared upward, a relic of powers he could not summon; the sight gave him hope, at the same time making him feel small. He felt anger in his humiliation, and turned quickly to follow Foler and Thessan before Anneka caught up to him.

Foler and Thessan were on their knees eating leaves from the sugarroot bushes. Ishbok sat down under a red-coned evergreen and picked a leaf from the nearest bush. Anneka was only a few paces behind him. She came up past him and sat down near the brothers without looking at him.

Ishbok swallowed the sweet juice and spit out the pulp. His stomach rumbled.

"Fabers!" Foler whispered loudly.

They all stood up and turned to look where he was pointing. On the angle of the mountainside, shapes stood among the evergreens, scaly manlike forms with long necks and slender tails.

Receding clouds let sunlight fall between the trees, scattering patches of bluish yellow on mossy rocks and soft earth. Somewhere a tree spook cried out and was still, reminding Ishbok of the colorfully plumed jack-dandies he had known as a child. In the silence of sun and shadow, the fabers began to move, stepping softly, surely, as if the evergreens had sprouted legs.

As the saurians moved in and out of sunlight, Ishbok saw the v-shaped mouths of the closest ones, set in the familiar grin; the golden eyes were wide under ridges, the skullcap crests suggesting the helmets of old time warriors from other times, other worlds.

But these fabers would not fight; they moved too slowly. These were not like the changed ones who had once fought for men. These were the dying ones, easy to kill and eat, yet they seemed to mock their destroyers.

Foler loosed his remaining good boomerang. It flew between the trees like a diving cinnamon bat and felled the forward faber. The creature tumbled down the incline while its companions stopped and switched their tails in agitation.

"Better than pig," Thessan said as he stopped the body's roll with his foot.

"We can cut it up and go home," Foler said.

Ishbok watched the single slit nostril of the dying faber as it drew in air in hungry rasps. The mouth was open, revealing the nearly human teeth set in a delicate jaw.

Thessan picked up a large rock and caved in the skull. When he stepped back the golden eyes were closed. The claw-tipped hands unclenched.

Ishbok looked up the mountainside, but the rest of the fabers were gone, leaving a mournful silence for the one who had died.

"Lucky it was not a killer pack," Foler said. He knelt down with Anneka and his brother. Together they began to cut up the body with their knives, selecting the best portions.

"We'll cut some hide to carry the meat in," Foler said.

Ishbok's stomach rumbled again, loudly enough to be heard. Foler laughed at the sound and continued cutting.

My knives, Ishbok thought. For Anneka the flesh meant a few days of life for her parents, and a more comfortable dying. Ishbok turned away as Thessan started to chew a piece of uncooked flesh.

"Here," Foler said. Ishbok turned to receive a wrapped cut of meat. "You carry one if you want to eat." *For Anneka's sake,* he told himself. "One day we'll find their eggs," Foler added.

A wind came up as the sun neared noon. It rushed through the trees like an angry thing. Red cones fell as if they were solid drops of blood. Ishbok thought that at any moment the wind would cry out in a shriek above its own fearful whispering.

As they marched back toward the city, Ishbok knew that he would eat the faber's meat with the others. His portion was not very heavy, but they were all weak from the morning's march; the meat held them together with its promise of rest. He would eat the meat as long as it was cooked, however badly.

Across the valley the city was a mirrored sheet of golden sunlight set against the hills, rising upward to a spear point in a blue sky. Ishbok wondered as he walked behind Foler and Thessan and Anneka. He tried to imagine all the things that he would never know—the skills which enabled men to live longer, heal their wounds, reach beyond the world.

He remembered reading about the giant city which sat on Charmian, moon-sister of the world; beings like himself had made a place for themselves there also. Others had travelled through the space between worlds, perhaps even to other stars.

Behind the city's spear point there was a large flat place where flying machines had once come to land, leaving off travellers and picking up new ones. He had seen a picture in a book. Long ago he had promised himself that he would climb up there, if he ever found the city. From that place, he had imagined, he would see more than anyone had seen in a long time.

Ishbok lay on his blankets in the corner of the room. Thessan was urinating on the small fire near the open window. The smell of burnt meat was still strong, despite the cool evening air drafting from the window through the door into the corridor. Anneka was with her parents, speaking softly to them. Foler lay on his blankets in the corner opposite from Ishbok. Anneka's parents had not been able to eat much. Half of the carcass was still uncooked.

"Fire's out," Thessan said.

The shadows of sunset seemed almost purple; the windows were panels of airy blue. Ishbok closed his eyes and saw the faber's face in the moment before the wise golden eyes had closed.

"Fire's out," Thessan repeated.

"Go to sleep," Foler said.

In time, Ishbok told himself, Anneka would belong completely to Foler and his brother. He saw himself moving on to another place, another group. If Anneka became heavy with Foler's child, that would be enough. Foler would lose an edgemaker: Ishbok would lose Anneka. *I have no courage,* he said to himself.

Ishbok opened his eyes and saw stars twinkling brightly in a darkening sky. His eyes were heavy. He felt uncaring in the tired satisfaction of his full stomach. Thessan had gone to lie down next to his brother. They were sleeping beasts and could not harm him. Faber faces mocked him when his eyes closed;

yet their expressions also seemed pitying. A dark tide came in upon him, billowing clouds of darkness carrying him away from all awareness.

II

Anneka's sobbing woke him near dawn. He lifted his head and saw her kneeling over her parents, a dark form against the pale light coming in through the windows.

He raised himself and crawled toward her, until he could see the old couple lying together in death. He got up on his knees and was still. Anneka did not look at him as she hovered over the lumpy masses of the dead.

Thessan began to snore loudly.

Ishbok knew that the old ones could not have lived much longer. Both had been more than thirty years old, though he had read that in the old time people had lived to a hundred. Even so the feeling of uselessness had contributed to their death.

In the corner beyond, Foler woke up to watch. Thessan began to snore even more loudly than before. Foler poked him in the ribs and the snoring stopped.

Anneka lay down next to her parents as if to imitate their stillness. In his corner Foler lay back and went to sleep. Ishbok moved backward on his knees and crawled under his blankets.

After a while sleep returned. Gratefully, he drifted away from the presence of death.

He awoke after what seemed a very long time, but the pale light of dawn was not much brighter than before. He sat up and looked around the room. Anneka was not with her parents. He peered across the room and saw her bare shoulders next to Foler's.

Ishbok got up on all fours and started to crawl toward her, his heart a cold stone in his chest. In a moment he saw that her dark eyes were open wide, staring at the ceiling as she clutched her portion of the gray blanket.

A whistle of air escaped from Thessan, who now slept a dozen paces away, like a dog who had been driven away for the night.

Ishbok stopped crawling. Anneka turned her head and looked at him, staring at him as if from out of a dark cave.

"Get away!" she whispered, baring her teeth grotesquely.

"Anneka..."

Foler awoke suddenly, saw him, and laughed.

"Swine," Ishbok said softly.

Foler propped himself up on one elbow and regarded him with mock seriousness. "If you weren't so useful I would kill you. Maybe I'd let Thessan do it."

"Go away," Anneka said. "Don't fight with him."

Ishbok stood up and said, "I'm leaving this morning."

Foler looked uncertain as he stood up wearing only his pants and boots.

Ishbok felt all his muscles tense as the thought of having been wrong about Anneka took hold of him. What did she see in Foler, who would lend her to his brother as easily as he would spit. He looked into her eyes, but they still stared at him from beyond the shadows.

Thessan awoke and giggled.

"You're not going to leave," Foler said. "I'll beat you into death first."

Anneka turned her face away from him.

"Filthy swine," Ishbok said, "you're no better than an animal."

Foler lunged at him, but Ishbok stepped to one side, turned and ran out the door into the corridor. Behind him Thessan was shrieking with glee.

Without stopping, Ishbok started to climb the stairway. He went up three stories without stopping.

His heart was pounding wildly when he stopped to listen. An acid taste had come up from his stomach. He threw up a little onto the black finished floor of the landing. He staggered toward the door which led into the city level and looked inside. Dark. He could not see inside.

Suddenly he heard a noise from below. Foler and Thessan were coming up after him. He turned in time to see Foler reach the landing, knife in hand.

Ishbok ran into the darkness of the room. As his eyes adjusted, he saw a door ahead of him, outlined in pale light. When he reached it a dark figure stepped into the frame. Ishbok heard Thessan's idiot laugh echo in the empty room. Somehow Thessan had reached this level by another way. The brothers were playing with him, he realized. He stopped and heard Foler come through the door behind him.

The thought of being beaten by Foler and Thessan was suddenly unbearable. Ishbok rushed toward Thessan's dark form. He bent low and knocked the shadow on its back with his head. The impact sent both of them sliding on the black floor until they came to a stop in the center of the next room.

Here the windows were gray with dawnlight. Ishbok saw another door at the far end as he scrambled to his feet. Thessan was clutching at him and shrieking. Ishbok kicked him in the ribs to free his right foot, and raced across the polished floor, out into the corridor and up the stairs. He heard Foler screaming at Thessan as he climbed, but when he paused on the next landing he heard only his own breathing.

"When I catch you," Foler shouted suddenly, "you'll never lech after a woman again!" His laugh echoed in the stair space.

Ishbok's one hope was to outlast the brothers in the climb. If he could get enough of a lead, then he could hide on one of the levels. They would not be able to guess where he had left the stairs.

He went up two more levels and stopped. Heavy footsteps chattered like curses from below. He took another deep breath and fled up the stairs, trying to step as lightly as possible.

One stretch of stairs, then another; a landing, the next stretch, a new landing, and the next. His bare feet were being burned by the friction of leather in his boots. After half a dozen turns he began to feel pain in his lungs. His heart was going to burst and his eyes would pop out of their sockets; he forced himself to the next landing and stopped.

He filled his lungs with air and held his breath for a few seconds, but the pulse of blood in his ears drowned all sound from below.

Gradually he heard the wheezing and labored breathing of the two men. Foler's curses grew louder, threatening to erupt as visible monstrosities; Thessan's high-pitched shrieks were snakes constricting the physical deformities conjured up in Ishbok's mind by Foler's wrath.

Foler's head appeared as he turned to climb the final stretch of stairs. Ishbok turned to climb higher and slipped on the polished surface before the first step. His forehead hit the fourth stair. He lay stunned, clawing at the railing.

In a moment the brothers were on him, collapsing on top of him in a heap. Foler was cackling. "Hold him down, Thes, then I'll cut it off and throw it down—"

Ishbok punched him in the face, and with a lucky thrust put a finger in Thessan's eye. Then he stood up, picking up the knife Foler had dropped.

As he went up the stairs, Ishbok dropped the knife down the stairwell. He reached the next landing and ran into the empty room. The one beyond it was bright with the orange light of the sun rising through the morning storm clouds. Ishbok passed into a third room. Here the windows were being dotted with the first rain drops of the storm. At the other end of the room he went through a door and found more stairs.

He went down two levels and hid in a windowless chamber. He tried to relax in the dark corner. If they caught up with him again, he would need all his strength. His best hope was that they were now as tired as he was, and would not want to waste the day. There was no food in the upper levels of the city; either Ishbok would come back or starve. If he tried to leave the city, they would be waiting. An upward climb would help him only briefly. Even if he could sneak past them into the countryside, they would track him like an animal. And today they would have food; tomorrow they would have food, while he would be weaker.

After a long while he got up, deciding that he would rather starve and die than be captured for the amusement of Foler and Thessan. They would humiliate him in front of Anneka, maiming and disfiguring him permanently. Then he would never be able to leave the group. He would not be able to hunt. He would grow old exchanging his skills for food and protection. They would force him to teach Anneka's sons. And when he was old and useless and empty of dreams, they would turn him out to die.

Anneka had never loved him; he had proof enough of that. But before he died, he would reach the top of the city. That much he could still accomplish; he would keep faith with his wish of long ago.

• • •

He fled upward for most of the morning, stopping to rest in dozens of rooms. The rain stopped and the sun rose with him, looking into the windows, lighting up his way, warming the chill of morning. He would stop occasionally to hear the sound of air coming up the stairwell, the sound of a breathing beast about to be loosed after him. The sight of Anneka with Foler would not fade from behind his eyes. His muscles were tight as he climbed; his mind held a naked hope, almost as if there would be some kind of answer at the top of the city, something so much greater than his life that it would destroy the hurt of the morning. He willed himself upward.

Finally, he came through the opening which led him out onto the flat area behind the great spire. He felt like a wanderer in a dream state. His lungs were heavy, his feet hurt, and he felt dizzy. The sun was hot on his face. It had won the race toward noon. The air was still and hot. He stopped to wipe the sweat off his face with the sleeve of his hide jerkin.

Ahead lay an open plain of metal. On it sat more than thirty aircraft from the old time, huge metallic birds, motionless. He walked toward them slowly, forgetting for a moment the reality of loss behind him.

He stopped beside one of the flying things and pulled himself up inside through an opening. He was inside a bubble-like window. He imagined that the craft was moving through the clouds, carrying him away from the city, freeing him of his prison.

His whole life had been a confinement. He would not have Anneka. There would be no children to weep over his death. He might have told them his dreams. Now there would be nothing.

He looked up at the blue sky. It was a desert of false promises, beckoning him on with unreal suggestions of worlds beyond; there was nothing there that could help him.

As his strength drained away, he sat back in the bubble. The climb had taken all his energy. There was no way to gain it back. Sleep was the only escape.

He woke up choking on the hot air trapped inside the bubble. The afternoon sun was a blinding fire in the sky, rousing him back to the struggle of his life. Death and his brother, sleep, fled before the eye of the sun called Caesar as he scrambled out of the aircraft.

A strong breeze cooled him. Huge clouds sat on the northern horizon, promising a storm by evening.

He walked to the edge of the city and looked out over the countryside of green hills and rocky outcroppings and the blue stream which twisted away to the hazy blue at the end of the world.

He looked down and saw three people moving away from the city. The figures were so small, so insignificant; he felt no interest in them. And he felt no hunger or thirst. His warm body drank the cool wind. He shivered and turned to walk back toward the flying machine. Perhaps he could rest under a wing.

He opened his eyes at night and the infinity of sky and stars had become a cage. The ring was a barrier, saying to him that he had climbed so far and would be permitted to go no higher. This plane of metal would be his grave, guarded by mechanical birds. The wind would blow away his flesh, the sun would bleach his bones; starlight would enter the open eyes of his stony skull to stir whatever ghosts of thought remained. He would lie here forever, as dead as his world, scarcely more dead than the life into which he had been born. Caesar would burn away, the veil of air would be torn from Cleopatra, all the time of passing would dwindle, but he would never come again.

Ishbok closed his eyes, looking for a semblance of peace within himself; now he found only weariness and hunger and hurt. He imagined the black wing of the aircraft moving down to cover him from the cold. Tears forced themselves out through his closed eyelids and he tasted their salt on his lips. The fever shivered his body.

Sleep came gently and he gave himself up to its calm.

III

Once, long ago, when he lay dying, a black dot appeared in the morning sky, growing larger as it came down until he screamed at its closeness. Then it crushed him and he had died.

Something strong held his head; his body was almost unfeeling. He opened his eyes. White, as if the very air were white. Black floaters in his eyes, flowing in and out of his direct vision. *Eye clouds,* his mother had called them, telling him to worry only if he saw one which did not move when he tried to look at it. Good food would always clear them up, and the same ones would not last more than a year.

He remembered light spilling out from an entranceway of some kind, like daylight but stronger, more like the white around him now. A strange thing sitting on the plane of metal . . .

Something was creating images in his brain, pushing him to think, changing him, prodding . . .

A man's garment reminded him of a mirror-wing moth, glittering. He sat in a small vessel, guiding it into a giant ship floating in the dark . . .

Time running backward . . . war fabers marching through snowy passes . . . across green fields . . .

An explosive burst of white light . . .

Plagues . . . piled bodies . . .

A world emptying out, subsiding into a terrible silence . . .

His world.

Reclaimed.

A word referring to him.

Others were being gathered from all over the world.

Slowly, thoughts became words, strange yet clear. Their meaning filled a need in him, one he had felt but never fully understood. Unfolding comprehension was wondrous, and frightening, as if the fiery sun itself were speaking to him.

". . . we have come to rebuild."

Suddenly he was rushing through space toward a yellow sun, and closer to linger over a blue world . . .

"Earth, the original home of your people and mine. The area of space within five hundred light years of Sol is dotted with failed colonies established more than a thousand years ago. Most are lingering near death. Our newest ships will link these worlds into a loose confederation. We have brought tools, generating plants which have the power of small suns. We have synthesis techniques to help you make all that is needed for life."

Ishbok opened his eyes and saw the woman's face. "Why should you want to do all this?"

"We wish to help," she said. Her hair was white, clinging to her head in short curls; her eyes were green. "A confederation benefits all who belong. It is better to live under law, in social and physical health; a confederation is better than being alone."

Ishbok thought of the food-gathering groups he had known, and how they depended on each other, suffering from need and at each other's hands.

"But why talk with me?"

She smiled. "Because I think you understand, and that will help you lead your people."

"Lead?"

"Rest now. There will be more to learn later." Her face receded into the white and a healing lethargy crept into his eyes, closing them.

He awoke feeling stronger than he had ever remembered; yet there was still a sense of struggle in his mind.

He knew so many new things, puzzling facts which he accepted without hesitation. The white room was in a giant starship circling Cleopatra. The starcrossing vessel was 10 kilometers long and capable of enormous velocities in excess of light speed. The offworlders had rebuilt his health. But he struggled with the thought of a device inside his head. "It will answer questions," the white-haired woman had told him. Answers to any question he might think, as long as there was an answer in the starship's memory elements. He did not always understand the answers. There was a strange new country inside him, as vast as all the libraries he had known, as complete as all the knowledge of humankind, the central homefire of a species.

He tried to sit up and the bed shaped itself to support him.

This new world will always be a part of you now, the woman had said.

Who were these offworlders who could see inside each other? Was it right for anyone to have such power?

"We are your brothers and sisters." The words were inside him, whispering across the presence of knowledge which suddenly seemed a precious gift.

"But that is how you want me to see it!" Ishbok shouted and sat up in his bed.

A door opened in the wall to his left, startling him. The woman with white curls walked in and sat down in the chair next to his bed.

"You've been debating with your tutor-link quite a lot, sometimes even in your sleep." She smiled again. "Let's be friends, Ishbok. My name is Hela Fenn. You can call me Fenn. My profession is psycho-soc. Do you have another name?"

Ishbok noted that she had known his name, but he did not remember giving it to her. "It's the only one," he said, wondering how much of himself was no longer his own.

"How's your understanding of incoming material? Do you get a full picture of why we are here?"

Ishbok nodded. "How old are you, Fenn?"

"I'm forty."

Almost twice Anneka's age, older in earth years. Older than anyone he had ever known.

"Everything we've learned about you, Ishbok, indicates strong mental abilities in a number of directions. You understand alternatives quickly, you know how much you can do and not do with the resources at hand; you will lead if given the chance, but you are willing to follow if you agree with one who leads—"

"How can you know these things? I don't even know them—"

"By your responses to dream strategies."

Ishbok felt a moment of fear.

"It's perfectly safe. Just like dreaming, except that certain decisive patterns are brought forward and reinforced."

"I don't like it and I don't want it ever again. And I don't know if I believe what you say about this tutor in my head. It seems to me that you may have the power to control my actions."

"Good," she said. "You're showing aggressively rational behavior. You'll need it to help your world."

He was about to object again, but he understood her.

"If you like," she said, "we can remove the link and give you an external head band—but that might be inconvenient. You might not have benefit when you most need it."

"Perhaps."

"Get dressed and we'll go to the observation deck. Later we'll shuttle down to your city and get you started."

"You make it sound easy."

"Only the travel part, Ishbok," she said as she stood up. "The rest will be difficult, and you may fail." She turned and went out through the opening door, leaving him with a feeling of suspicion and apprehension.

Ishbok looked out into night and stars. Cleopatra glowed in blues and golds and browns, veiled in silvery clouds, encircled by the diamond dust of the ring, faceted debris and sculpted moons. Screens in back of him let in the light of Caesar; others showed space in various directions from the starship.

My world, he thought. *Nowhere is its suffering visible.*

"I'm sorry to be late," Hela Fenn said. He turned around as she was sitting down in one of the lounge chairs. She pointed to a seat opposite her own and put one foot up on the low table in the middle. "Sit down, Ishbok."

He noticed her clothes for the first time. One-piece green suit, wide pants, half boots. The garment came up around her neck in a tight fit.

"Do you really care?" he asked as he sat down.

"How do you mean?"

"My world—do you really care about helping?"

"I could give you a purely emotional answer which might please, but that would be to go against my convictions. Yes, we care, but we will all gain economically and socially. We are all Earth peoples. More than a thousand years ago, the home planet cast off its innovators, malcontents, idealists, dreamers—whatever name can be attached to them. A period of turmoil and cultural sterility followed, one which is not yet completely over. And this decline was mirrored in the history of every colony world we have visited. The colonists took bits and pieces of Earth with them, including all the old problems, and it shows in the state of every colony world we've seen.

"As nearly as we can make out from a year of investigation, the following is what happened on Cleopatra since the arrival of humankind more than a thousand years ago. A world grew in all directions from the place of landing. People grew different from one another; they moved away to create different places. The world filled up. Cleopatra changed. The local flora and fauna retreated before the life from Earth." She paused for a moment. "It's been coming back recently, but the world is a hybrid. Two kinds of fabers exist now, where once there was only one. At first fabers were modified to be workers and servants, and performers—dancers, musicians; they were also research animals. The warlike fabers hunt the original fabers, and men hunt them both.

"Anyway, the emerging nations grew apart. There were small wars and large wars; eventually a few small nations dragged Dardania and Pindaria, the largest powers, into a war involving biological weapons. It ended with a nuclear holocaust. The only good thing about the use of atomic weapons in those final days was that their use was confined to a few large cities and against military bases."

It's going to start all over, he thought, *unless we could become . . . something else, perhaps something that did not live on worlds where even simple things were lacking . . .*

". . . but enough has remained to start again."

"This ship is almost a small world, isn't it, Fenn?"

"You can think of it that way. It's as large as many cities were in the past, in the centuries before space travel."

He looked directly at her for a moment.

"Is anything the matter, Ishbok?" Her look was helpful, serious, without guile.

"I'm wondering about what I have come to, if it is possible for me to be right."

"You're one of the ones Cleopatra needs." She spoke without a trace of hesitation.

"Why are you so sure—what do you know that I can't see?"

"I see what you will see when you find yourself in the reality of leading. You will know what to do, or you will not."

He stood up and turned away from her to look at the sight of Cleopatra. *They are all planning this,* he thought. *They think I will inevitably choose what they will agree with. What if I do things they cannot support? Surely they must know I am having doubts? Still, I cannot let the chance pass to stand between my people and these offworlders. I cannot let so much opportunity go by. She's right. I can help.*

He looked at the planet swimming in the starry void. *To them my world is an island.*

"I'll be with you to help, Ishbok," Hela Fenn said behind him. "I know what you must be feeling."

You may know too much, he thought. He wondered if they were capable of killing him; or if they were truly so wise as to know all the needs of his world, and his own.

He noticed then that she was standing next to him. There was a restrained pride in her stance, unlike anything he had ever seen in another person.

"If it will help you to know," she said, "there are those on Earth who oppose all the help we are trying to administer among the failing colonies. Our compromise with them is to let native leaders take the major role, whenever we can. To do nothing would be cruelty, don't you think?"

"I feel hopeful about what you say," he said, "but I must see more." *My world, my world, I pledge myself to you. I will do the best I know how, the best I can learn . . .*

"To be honest," she said, "there is some vanity in it."

Swirling clouds rushed up at the shuttle, replacing the sight of oceans and land with obscurity. *To come back and be so close,* he thought, *makes my world all the universe there is again.* He sat watching the forward screen in the passenger section of the shuttle. Hela Fenn sat next to him.

Soon the clouds broke and he saw the landing area of the city far below. The city grew larger.

"There will be a crowd," Hela Fenn said. "You know what to expect?"

"Yes."

"We're drifting down on gravs now. Try and smile when the crowd cheers. It's important to have them like you. Almost a quarter of all remaining human life has been gathered into this city since you've been gone. Do you feel the role you will play, my friend? Can you see your children and their future?"

He felt alone. "What will come must be better than what I grew up in." The crowd was looking up at him through the screen. The old air machines were gone, cleared by the off-worlders. He missed the old hulks.

The shadow of the circular shuttle grew smaller on the

landing surface. The screen went dark as they touched, but went on again to show faces peering into the passenger section. Ishbok noted that they were mostly young faces—men and women looking newly washed and fed, and cautious in their expressions.

Hela Fenn led the way out between the empty seats. Ishbok followed her to the center of the cabin. They stood together on the lift plate which dropped them down into the airlock.

The lock was already open, the oval exit framing the crowd outside. Hela stepped out first. Ishbok followed and stood next to her at the top of the ramp. The shuttle was a ceiling above them, casting a shadowy circle. Beyond the circle the crowd stood in Caesar's light.

Ishbok searched the faces of the closest ones, the unfamiliar faces filled with hope.

"One of your own!" Hela said, her voice booming from amplification and bouncing in the space under the shuttle. "He knows what Cleopatra needs; he knows what you need; he knows what the city needs. He will carry our help to you. Go to him, talk with him, tell him what can be done."

The crowd cheered. The sunlight seemed brighter.

"Soon the city's water, heat and light will be working fully. You will be able to farm the countryside; and later we will show you how to live without agriculture. These are material things only. Your task will be to educate yourselves, administer laws, reconciling all the differences between yourselves, the process which makes a state necessary." She stopped speaking. "Now, let's go down among them," she whispered.

Anneka's face caught him from the center of the crowd. He stood frozen, afraid, naked in his new clothes. Then he noticed Foler and Thessan standing next to her. *They don't recognize me*, he thought. Anneka seemed bewildered.

"We'll go through the crowd and down to your office and living quarters a floor below," Hela whispered. "You must go first."

Ishbok walked down the ramp, all the while staring at Anneka. When he reached the bottom of the ramp, he was too low to see her in the throng. Fenn was next to him. They walked forward.

The cheering resumed as the crowd parted for him. He

walked ahead trying to smile as hands grasped at him and slapped his shoulders.

A man stepped in front of him. Ishbok recognized Foler—cleaner, shaved, dressed in offworlder fabrics, he was still surviving in his own way.

"What did you have to do to get all this, fool?"

You'll be opening a new period of history. The words chased each other through his brain. *Cleopatra will become a crossroads of interstellar commerce and cultural exchange.*

"You had better step aside," Hela Fenn said. "If this crowd hears you they'll tear you apart. Back off."

Foler stepped aside, his face mocking them. Ishbok hurried past him, through the rest of the crowd, and down a half-familiar flight of stairs. Hela Fenn was at his side as they came out into a lighted passage.

She walked ahead of him down the corridor, past one open door after another. Ishbok glimpsed workmen rebuilding the interiors. She stopped in front of a large door at the end. It slid open and he followed her inside.

"This is where you will live and work." The room was carpeted in soft green. A desk stood in the alcove of three windows, giving him an unobstructed view of the surrounding countryside.

"Come, sit down behind your desk," she said. She sat down in one of the chairs facing it. He sat down and looked at her.

"We're an empty world," he said, "which might be turned to advantages I can't guess yet."

"I picked you as one who would question and object," she said.

"On the way down you were telling me about history. Could you continue, Hela? I was very interested."

"I was talking about the need to break out of the cycles of prosperity and decline—the general rule among civilizations, at least the human ones we've seen."

"Are there others?"

"We don't know yet, but we're sure there are. Anyway, part of the answer lies in the use of vast resources, far beyond the kind available on a single planet. A single solar system is a good industrial base. The struggle then passes from a filling of material needs to a development of internal resources, the inner satisfactions of a human being. That part we don't fully understand yet. What we are fairly certain of is that there is no absolute necessity for the rise and decline of cultures. There may be a way out."

"What if you're wrong? What if it's always birth, decay, death, and new beginning. I see it in the man who stopped me outside, Foler."

"The new courts will deal with him."

"Can the courts take away his hatred of me? Can they remove his desire to mutilate me with a knife?"

Ishbok saw the pained expression on Hela's face. "I know you've seen a lot of darkness. But the light is there. We have to try."

Ishbok wondered if Anneka had gone to Foler out of choice, or to save the blademaker's life. Perhaps Foler had told her to play up to him so he would keep on producing tools; perhaps she even loved Foler.

"We're hoping that those like yourself, Ishbok, will have enough internal resources to resist decline."

"I cannot live forever. The time of those like Foler will come again." He smiled at her, feeling his own bitterness. "But I will try, Hela, I will try." *Anneka, did you save my life, even once?*

"Later . . . we'll send you a few security experts, Ishbok. They will help you train your own police force. There will also be experts who will help you run the city, including the schools, which will help create your own teams."

"Will my police carry weapons?"

"Harmless ones—the kind that can stop but not kill." She paused. "You will have enemies. The power will be yours to use. You will have to control it."

He saw Foler with a spear in his chest. Thessan hurtling to his death from the top of the city.

"I'm afraid of my thoughts, Hela, maybe you were wrong about me."

"If anything you convince me more. You're a kind, concerned man, one who would never seek power; therefore you are the one who must use it. You will form a government and you will govern."

Suddenly the words ran out between them. *I can never be*

one of the offworlders, his thoughts continued. *I've never belonged to any of the groups I've known. I've always been alone, holding back.* The awkward silence was a prison, an equilibrium of agreement and disagreement between Hela and himself. *And I am not completely a Cleopatran either.*

As if in answer, Hela Fenn said, "You will be the first of the new Cleopatrans. Let me tell you the story of Cincinnatus the Roman . . ."

IV

In the first months of mayorship, the representatives of the various groups gathering in the city came to talk with him; the captain of the starship paid a call, as did many volunteers from earth. The representatives confused him; the captain made him suspicious; the volunteers brought the skills he needed, so he put them to work. There were so many details in the doing of things that he almost forgot who he was.

"Leadership is being the center of a storm," Hela said in the second month. He was more interested in getting things done than in theorizing about them. There was more worry in thoughts than he could carry from day to day.

In the third month Foler raped one of the women volunteers from the starship, a medic. He held his own brother as a hostage to avoid capture by the police, and killed Thessan before surrendering. The trial which Ishbok had thought could be avoided was held. He did not attend and refused to have anything to do with it, although he might have been one of the three judges who heard the case.

"He grew up surviving," Hela had said to him. "He knows no other life and never will. His sense of inadequacy is complete in the new way of things, where nothing is open to him through the cruel means he knew in the past."

"I did not learn those ways."

"Your parents, Ishbok."

He sighed. "What will be the sentence?"

"We can retrain him, wipe memories, initiate new behavior and value patterns."

"You might just as well kill him—it's the same when you

take away identity and memory."

"You could imprison him, or kill him instead. We'll do what we know how only with your permission, and if the court agrees."

"I don't know, Hela, I'll have to think." *Kill him! He's hopeless.*

"Let the courts decide," she said, "you're too close. If your courts don't have this power of decision, you'll have a world of power by individuals with no reference to laws."

The conversation had made him angry. The remembered rigamarole had not resulted in a solution for him. In a moment Anneka would come into his office. She was four months pregnant with Foler's child.

The door slid open. She came in and sat down in the chair in front of the desk. "I've come," she said, "to ask you not to kill Foler."

"I've made no plans to kill him, Anneka." *Anneka,* his thoughts whispered softly.

"And I want you to understand, more than anything," she continued without looking at him. "I chose him because I love him. But I would have chosen him anyway, because he was strong and would protect our children." She looked at him with tears in her eyes. "You are for another world. I tried to attract you so you would stay and make knives and points—I like you, but not as a lover or a father. I'm sorry, but don't kill him. I won't know what to say to his son."

"What if it's a daughter?"

"It will be a son," she said. A world of brutality stood behind her words, all of Foler's defiance and will, and she still lived in its service. *I could not be a father to her children,* Ishbok thought, *but I can be a protector of my city and my world.*

"He may not die, Anneka, but he may return . . . changed. It will not be my decision, but the court's."

She looked at him with doubt. "You let others make your choices—how can you be a man?"

"Don't you see, the same law must apply to all. I cannot decide. If I do, it will be meddling." *I'm not really sure,* he thought, *but I must decide.*

She stood up with restrained hatred in her eyes and spit at his desk.

She came to manipulate me again, he thought as Anneka turned and went out. The door slid shut and he sat in the silence of the room, listening to the sound of his pulse pounding in his ears, marking his own rising hatred, not only of Anneka and Foler, but of everything from which he had sprung.

The sooner it was swept away the better...

In the evening Ishbok was alone in the silence of the blood-red sun. He looked out across the valley at the deep blue shadows cast by the setting sun, and wondered about the future.

He tried to imagine this confederation, this greater world into which his wayside world would emerge. What battles, what disagreements would be possible there? What cycles of birth, decay and death, and new beginnings lay ahead for a civilization spanning the stars? How many isolate worlds were there tucked away in the miserable corners of the universe? He wondered if Cleopatra had better been left unfound, lost among the grains of stars, to rebuild by itself from its family squabbles rather than be shamed by intruders from the stars.

But he knew that it would be impossible now for him to see Cleopatra as the whole world; he had seen his home from beyond the sky, a glowing sphere set in a night of stars. He had seen its oceans, its land, the ring sweeping around the planet like unwanted riches being cast off into the void. He had looked down into the dark hemisphere where this city lay, invisible; he had seen it light up in the night, coming back to life after a thousand years.

Cleopatra circled Caesar, and Caesar was only one star among a countless number, yet all the importance of his life lay here. His own people would mistrust him, and he would mistrust the off-worlders; there was no safety in the thought. He would not be able to forget all that was; he would do his best to affect what would be.

Now he would have to be more than a warrior or a hunter or a craftsman, or a father; he would have to be a ruler, a helper.

The sun slid halfway behind the horizon. *I will have to learn to speak to my own people, as well as I speak with Hela. My children will have to know more than I do.* He thought of the many world histories belonging to the other worlds of the sky.

He would ask Hela for them. Maybe there would be something he could learn from such a study. There were other reclaimed worlds entering the confederation. He tried to picture new, unspoiled worlds circling distant suns . . .

He thought of Anneka and her child. He wondered how the city would react to Foler's coming sentence, whatever that would be.

The sun was down. Stars appeared in the sky. Below him city light spilled out into the valley. The ring cut a swath in the sky, a carpet preparing the way for chunky Charmian to rise and overtake Iras. Clouds sat on the northern horizon, promising a storm by morning. A black-winged deltasoar sailed into the twilight.

Ishbok stood up, sighing, knowing what he would do. He would govern with all the help there was to be had. He had become someone else, a stranger who would daily startle his earlier self; there was terror in the thought.

He knew that he would be lonely.

The Monadic Universe

"Looking back through the computer-enhanced electronic telescope," the voice from the screen said, "the solar system is wrapped in a shimmering field—as you can see—which nothing in normal space can penetrate. It can best be described as a field-disruption anomaly of some kind—a terrifying quirk in the electromagnetic-gravitational continuum of near-sun space. Inside the anomaly physical laws are gradually becoming more indeterminate, and no reversal or halt to this tendency is expected.

"It is assumed that your three ships exited the anomaly safely through hyper-space. Contact with myself and those still alive on earth is now impossible. There is no way to determine exactly how much time earth has before the end. Now you must act as if your three ships are all of humanity."

The picture on the screen changed and a woman's voice continued the narration. The view showed a dense starfield. "It is believed," the female voice said, "that this region of space, twenty thousand light years toward the galactic center, is filled with earthlike planetary systems relatively close together. Though transit time via hyper-space has never been accurately measured from point to point, to give us a yardstick, it is estimated that it will take at least eight decades to reach the target area utilizing current technology; this is still an improvement over transit via normal space. The perfection of drive systems is a matter for your future.

"We did not choose a closer target because suitable targets are more scarce in near-sol space; and, looking toward your future, our planners decided that it would be worth the effort to establish multi-system colonies at once—to insure humankind's survival, cultural differentiation and—"

Rescher cut the sound from his headset and watched the visual without commentary. The star plate of the region of space which had been their destination for the last three decades was thick with stars, to the point where certain areas looked like sheets of light. He looked at massive areas of interstellar dust which blocked out the starlight. He knew he should feel hopeful, but he looked with no emotion at the small screen in the library cubicle. He knew that around the massive egg-shaped hull of the starship the gray nothingness of hyper-space was infinite, unlike the curved structure of normal space-time; and he felt grateful for the visual tie-in with normal space which enabled him to look out into a lighted void hung with the lanterns he knew as stars. He thought of the starship as an old sailing vessel moving within sight of land, fearful of venturing out to sea, out of sight of land, perhaps to fall off the edge of the world . . .

The program was over, the screen was blank. Rescher stretched his arms and yawned. He listened to the silence, to the almost subliminal hum of the ship. Somewhere, he knew, Captain Hoyt had been wakened from long-sleep and was preparing to make his once-a-decade rounds; elsewhere Jay Dunn was awake and probably dreaming up trick questions to ask the computer to see if it was still sane, not merely logical. Sanity in this case was defined by human interest and a pragmatic concern with human well-being. After all, the main cybernetics were in charge of more than two thousand lives, half of them still unborn. The ship had been built for survival, all the half-mile-long, egg-shaped bit of it, a microcosm carrying samples of all earth's major life forms, the sum total of human knowledge and culture. All this the earth had thrown in the abyss, humankind's last bid for immortality.

Except for the visual tie-in with normal space, the ship was isolated, even from its two sister ships. Rescher hoped, for the third time in three decades, that the other ships had made it safely out of the solar system; he closed his eyes and tried to reach out with his hope, tried to visualize Rita on one of the other ships, and know that she was alive, that he would see her again under a new sun and sky. He didn't know which ship she was on; each ship was the same and each was nameless. Each had been completed at a different time, and he had made Rita go on the first one. No one had taken the trouble to name the ships later on. It was as if a special kind of modesty, a superstition really, would somehow enable humankind's ships to slip past fate's gaze to safety.

He remembered that last night on earth, now thirty years in the past. Rita had already gone. He remembered the strange electrical storm dancing across a night sky in which stars were streaks instead of points; he knew that it should *seem* as if it was only yesterday. He had awakened only three times since the ship had entered hyper-space, and time past should seem like only three nights to him; yet it seemed to him that he *felt* every year of those three decades, despite the artificially induced deep sleep which had been designed to produce dreamless slumber. He felt the ship's isolation in the formless unreality of the alien plenum; he felt the ship's emptiness of humanity; he thought of the endless corridors opening into the central hold of the ship where the sleepers rested, waiting to be reborn.

He got up and left the cubicle. In the hallway only the dim footlights were on. He coughed and listened to his echo. He crossed the hall and stepped into the empty elevator. A few moments later it let him off in front of one of the two screen lounges on the top deck. He walked in slowly, still a bit groggy from sleep, and sat down in a reclining chair in the row against the wall. The empty chairs sat with him, staring at the three blank rectangles which were the observation screens. He pushed a button on his right armrest and they lit up.

The universe was there; it could be counted on: three rectangles littered with stars. The left screen showed the view aft, where the stars trailed off into nothingness between the island galaxies. The right screen showed a rotating view of space, seen from the largest circumference of the egg-shaped vessel. The middle screen was an open immensity into which the starship fled.

The computer adjusted tie-in with normal space made the stars still look like stars; and it corrected the view constantly in relation to normal space as the ship ate up distance toward the galactic center. The view was enhanced, but it was the view of their route as it would appear if the ship had been moving in space-time, slowed down for the perceptions of the human nervous system. He was glad they had been able to make these screens work after all the trouble in design; they broke the ship's isolation in hyper-space. Otherwise the screens would have shown only the empty, unformed grayness: the eyes of a dead man.

He felt restless. The very thought of the ship made him restless. He wanted to break out. He needed a world, a sun and sky, wind and weather; all the things of an earth he would never see again. They would not be the same elsewhere.

After two more sleep periods he would be able to wake up more people; by the end of the eighth period the entire ship's crew of one hundred technicians would be up and ready to wake the colonists. Two more *nights* of sleep and he would be able to talk to others besides Hoyt and Dunn; but sleeptime was now a full month away and his restlessness worried him.

He remembered how he and Rita had played together at the Farside Lunar Base. Ley Crater had a big gym dome with a heavily padded floor three hundred feet in diameter, and he pictured her slim form jumping after his stocky body in the great space of the dome. He remembered her laughter; he remembered how a much younger Dunn had enjoyed watching them together from the observation deck. He remembered how Hoyt would break the magic spell with his business-like manner when he came to drag them all back to their job. He always came early.

On the middle screen the ship was rushing toward a great mass of stars; toward a billion suns rushing through dust clouds, unaware of the tiny gnat from earth. Actually the ship was a ghost in normal space-time and invisible. His thoughts wandered and for a moment he did not notice that the stars on the right screen were gone. A face appeared and smiled at him. A large hand pressed on the outside of the middle screen. The hand became a fist and smashed the screen and reached in from the outside to grab him. He jumped from his chair and moved back toward the door. He felt sweat running down his back underneath the green coverall he was wearing. As he watched, the hand withdrew and the screen became whole again; but the face on the right screen was laughing—the face of a woman with classical features and long brown hair. Then in a wink it too disappeared and the screens showed the view aft and side and the forward rush of the ship.

Rescher found Captain Guillaume Hoyt sitting alone in the large mess hall, drinking soup out of the same large mug that he would later use for coffee. Hoyt was a tall man and he had to lean down to the table as he sat. He held his elbows on the table, keeping the mug close to the chiseled features of his face. Captain Hoyt was the only member of the crew with whom Rescher was not on a first name basis. Hoyt himself addressed people by their first or last names as it pleased him, it seemed. Rescher sat down opposite to him and nervously told what he had seen.

Hoyt downed the rest of his soup and put the empty mug down on the polished metal of the table. "You're half asleep, Frank." Then he rubbed his crew-cut brownish-blond hair with the palm of his left hand.

"I'm all right," Rescher said.

"Get something to drink, or eat. I recommend it," Hoyt said.

"Look," Rescher said, "we can run back the screen record up in the control section."

Hoyt looked directly at him, seemingly more alert. "You're not jesting, are you, Rescher?"

"No, I'm not," Rescher said, trying to look his most serious.

"I suggest that we go check it," Hoyt said. He stood up, dwarfing Rescher in his chair. Even when Rescher stood up to follow him out of the hall, the Captain was a head taller.

They went down the way between a row of fifty tables, all chairless except for the one they had been sitting at, and stepped

out into the hallway where the footlights stretched away into
the vanishing point and the center of the ship. The elevator
was only fifty feet down the hall. As he walked toward the
open door Hoyt said over his shoulder to Rescher, "Dunn is up
in the control area now." In the elevator going up he continued,
"Something might be wrong with the tie-in to normal space. I
suggest we check it, then you."

"I'm all right," Rescher said.

"I suggest we wait. Dunn might be playing a practical joke.
It wouldn't be too hard to program any kind of visual into the
screens."

"I *don't* think that's it," Rescher said. He had raised his
voice slightly to the Captain. He shut up. In the silence he
knew that he had reached Hoyt enough to worry him.

II

The tie-in mechanism with normal space-time was a black box
six feet long and four feet tall. It was located a deck below the
control area. The room was small. The light flashed on into a
harsh electric blue as the three men walked in and the door
slid shut behind them. They stood in front of it for a few
moments, trying to make some sense from its outward appearance. Finally Dunn walked slowly around the box and
stopped on the other side. Rescher remembered the look on
both Hoyt's and Dunn's faces as they had played back the
record of the tie-in visual since the start of their waking watch.
Jay Dunn, the youngest of the three, had shaken his head and
said, "Ridiculous, something's messing our reception somewhere."

Rescher looked at him now as he walked around the black
box. Dunn scratched the back of his head, twisted his light
moustache and said, "This thing here channels and organizes
our visual contact with normal space into the screen. I wonder
what could be wrong with it?"

"You're the physicist," Hoyt said. He seemed to be taking
all of this as a personal affront.

"Yeah, I know that," Dunn said looking up at the tall man.

"I know how to *fix* things, which is why I get to wake up a lot, but if this involves more theory than I can handle we'll have to get help from the stiffs below, or I spend a lot of time in the library asking questions until I get the right answers."

"It's got to be here, Jay," Rescher said. "The Captain and I both saw what we saw on the screens. It's here that something is wrong."

"Hey," Dunn said, smiling, "you two wouldn't be pull—" He stopped in midword, and Rescher could see by the expression on Dunn's face that he didn't believe it was a gag.

Captain Hoyt was shaking his head, apparently unamused by Dunn's words. Rescher saw a moment of confusion in Dunn's face, as if the younger man feared possible failure in his assigned tasks.

"The problem is real," Rescher said. But this seemed to make Hoyt even more impatient.

"That cable on the floor; where does it go?" Hoyt said, pointing to it.

"Into the computer in the control section," Dunn said. "I can ask the computer some diagnostic questions to start . . . I guess we should get up there. But I wonder why the computer hasn't started screaming alarm at us by now . . ."

Rescher looked at the black box sitting there, a mysterious mass on the floor, and felt suspicious of it. Everything the ship saw in normal space depended on it. If it failed the screens would fade to show the gray nothingness of other-space, the terrifying vastness beyond familiar reality, an infinite limbo which could swallow them all up in its endless unreality . . .

"Come on, you two," Hoyt said and turned to the door. It slid open for him. They went out after him.

The computer was singing a high sing-song when Rescher came into the control room behind Dunn and Hoyt. The control area was an ultra-lighted room a hundred and fifty feet square. When fully staffed it would hold twenty-five crew members. There were four oversize screens, one on each wall. The computer console was located beneath the forward screen opposite the wall where the sliding doors which gave entrance were situated. Together now, the three men sat down in three of the station posts in front of the console. Captain Hoyt crossed his long legs and put his elbows heavily on the armrests. Dunn sat forward and placed his fingers near the operations controls. Rescher sat back and took a deep breath.

Dunn began punching buttons. The computer cut short its sing-song and gave out a monotone mid-range tone.

"Standard check," Dunn said, "I'll have it answer on audio as well as on printout."

The monotone signal changed into a recognizable voice which shaped its words with faultless precision:

ALL UNITS OPERATIONAL
EXPECTED EFFICIENCY
NO MALFUNCTIONS

"Check tie-in with normal space-time," Dunn said slowly.

UNIT WORKING AS DESIGNED
NO MALFUNCTIONS

"Look, Jay," Rescher said suddenly, "ask *how* it works."

"Describe how the unit functions," Dunn said. "Use elementary terms." He gave Rescher a questioning look, a serious looking pout, Rescher thought. Rescher looked past him to Captain Hoyt who sat clutching his elbows now and leaning toward the colored pilot lights on the panel with the usual stoic look on his Germanic face. He did not know the man at all, Rescher realized. The Captain's inner workings seemed distant and unimaginable, even though they were probably fairly ordinary. Dunn could be reached regularly, by the simplest words or behavior; but Hoyt was a citadel against the whole universe.

The computer gave its answer:

THE TIE-IN IS NOT A TRUE VISUAL CONTACT WITH NORMAL SPACE-TIME
IT IS A SIMULATION BUILT UP OUT OF RELIABLE DATA
ALL THREE SHIPS WERE PROGRAMMED WITH THE SAME SIMULATION A SENSORY EXTRAPOLATION OF THE VISUAL ROUTE TO THE TARGET AREA

IT WAS NOT POSSIBLE TO SIMULATE CRED-
IBLE CONTACT WITH THE OTHER TWO SHIPS
  NO OTHER CONTACT WITH NORMAL SPACE-
TIME IS POSSIBLE
  SEE STANDARD FILE ENTRY FOR DETAILS OF
THIS PROGRAM AND ITS INCEPTION

Dunn said, "It was telling the exact truth when it said the
unit was functioning as *per design.*"

"A ploy to keep us happy," Captain Hoyt said softly.

"They left it for us to find out, *if* we asked the right questions," Dunn said.

"But still," Rescher said, "we know what I saw and none
of this explains that."

"Anyway, our black box is in *fine* working shape," Dunn
said with derision. He gave a hopeless sigh and sat back in his
seat.

Captain Hoyt turned in his seat and said, "Anything that
damned thing shows us will be approved by the computer.
What do you two make of it?"

"Maybe it's to keep us on our toes," Rescher said.

"It is a pretty good view, after all," Dunn said.

"I can see why they thought they had to do it," Hoyt said.
"They had to let us know gently, and still keep the goal before
us. I think there's more to this."

Rescher knew he was right. He imagined how it would be
without the view on the screens—a blank wall of gray for the
stiffs to face as they woke up. On earth they had decided not
to take even the slightest chance with the future of humanity—
what was left of it. *Keep them busy,* the psychs had said, or
something like it. If a few of them go poking behind the scenes,
let them find out. They may not tell the rest, and again they
may. They might laugh at our management, laugh and go on
their own way. *Get through! Survive.* What more could there
be to this?

Next to him Dunn leaned forward suddenly, punched a tab
and asked, "Give more details, search the library."

THE SIMULATION IS A GOOD LIKENESS OF
THE WAY TO THE TARGET AREA

PROBABILITY IS NEAR NINETY PER CENT
THAT THE MODEL AND THE REALITY RESEM-
BLE EACH OTHER
A DIFFERENCE WHICH MAKES LITTLE DIF-
FERENCE CAN IN THIS CASE BE IGNORED

"Can the simulator be turned off?" Dunn asked.

YES
IT IS NOT ADVISABLE IN TERMS OF ASSUMP-
TIONS OF DESIGN
THE MAIN UNIT CAN BE DISCONNECTED
FROM THIS COMPUTER BY DIRECT ORDER OR
BY DETACHING THE CONNECTING CABLE

"What—what will we see on the screens?" Rescher noticed
the nervousness in Dunn's voice. Hoyt shifted in his seat.

NOTHING
AN INDETERMINATE PLENUM
AN UNDEFINED CONTINUUM

"What is our presence in this plenum? Do we have any
effect?"
The computer took thirty seconds to answer. Captain Hoyt
cracked his knuckles and shifted in his seat again.

WE CREATE SPACE SEMI-SPACE WITH THE
SHIP'S PRESENCE
MORE FACTS CAN BE DEDUCED IN TERMS OF
EARTH DERIVED DATA CONCERNING SPATIAL
CONCEPTS

"I don't know what else I can ask," Dunn said looking at
Rescher and then at Hoyt.
"There would be no point in turning it off," Hoyt said. "It
is all we have. A rough progress map, but the only one."
"We can never know just how real the simulation is," Rescher
said. "We have to take the computer's word for it, and they
could easily have programmed it to say what we *need* to hear."

"We will leave it on," the Captain said as he stood up to his full height. "Let's see if we get any more freak sights on the screens. Rescher, you go up to the library consoles and look up the standard file on this whole thing which the computer mentioned. There may be much more to this. Come back with what you find. Dunn, finish your regular rounds. Gentlemen, I was the first one up this decade and I'm going to get some regular sleep."

"I'll do it now," Rescher said.

Jay Dunn left the control section. Hoyt sat down again at his computer station and looked at Rescher. "Frank," he said, smiling, "maybe the whole universe is some kind of shadow play run by some kind of extra-cosmic black box?" The Captain didn't look right to Rescher. How long has he been awake, a year, five years? Does he take his long-sleep regularly? The lines in his face were deep. Doesn't he want to get where we're all going? Rescher thought.

"That would be mind-boggling, Captain." Hoyt didn't answer, but sat back in his chair, seeming very tired; and as Rescher looked at him, he felt his own suspicions, shapeless as they still were, reinforced.

III

"Whoever you are, listening to this now—I must tell you that we had to keep what I'm going to tell you from you so that you would make the attempt, at least, to leave the solar system. You might not have left otherwise." The old man on the screen in the library cubicle spoke very deliberately, with a voice which seemed too forceful for his old frame. "I hope only one person is listening to this, three at most. If you are *one* listening to this, then try to understand, son, that you must tell the others carefully, perhaps not at all. You know now that the visual tie-in with normal space is a kind of sham. But there is something more important."

Suddenly Rescher hated the old man on the screen. He hated him and all the planners who had made it so easy for him and all the sleepers to toss their lives into a gray nothingness, tricked by the promise of *seeing* the promised land on the screens throughout the journey. His palms became sweaty as he gripped the armrests of the chair.

". . . a problem you will have to face concerning the nature of hyper-space," the old man was saying. The skin on his face appeared to be almost transparent. Rescher could tell he was in pain, as the insides of his body slowly fell apart, functioned less and less well within the field of the system-wide anomaly. Rescher felt dread at the thought of further words from the figure on the screen.

"No ship has ever shifted into hyper-space and come back out without acquiring a deadly kind of energy-potential, which caused the ship to be torn apart upon re-entering the normal continuum. The unfortunate thing about all this is that we suspect that the solar anomaly which now isolates the solar system from the rest of the galaxy was triggered by our experiments with hyper-spatial drives. And, as it turned out afterward, the only way to leave the solar system after the onset of the anomaly was through hyper-space. We had to *make* you leave this way, or humanity would not survive at all. So we set up a program by which you would discover all the problems for yourself—and hopefully the solutions. Exactly how you have been led to listen to me I will never know. These are terrible things I'm saying, I know, but there was no other way that we could believe in. Everything we know is in your computer banks. Use it, add to your data if possible, and begin your computer analysis—begin from as many starting points as suggest themselves to you."

The screen faded, leaving Rescher with his fears. He knew that the old man was probably dead—no, surely dead. He tried to visualize how it must have been on earth during those last days, when reality itself was falling apart, and all the commonplace ways of nature no longer held. Normal metabolic functions could no longer be trusted; the simplest foods would very often kill. World-wide famine. And at night the sky was filled with streaks, smudged stars, and strange lights—the signs of rival forces struggling for dominion over the earth. During the days millions of eyes watched the heavens, but this time it was no mere eclipse, but the sight of a dull red sun, enormously flattened at both poles and dotted with sunspots, another sign of the cancerous wrinkling of space-time which would soon obliterate them all. The vision still managed to stagger Rescher's imagination: the completely unpredictable unknown had swallowed the entire solar system. Like a frog swallowing a fly.

In the mess hall Captain Hoyt stared into his food as he ate. Dunn sipped a drink. Rescher buttered a piece of synthetic bread slowly. Hoyt and Dunn had been stunned after he had told them the situation. The ship might be the only reality they would ever know.

"I'm scared out of my wits," Jay Dunn said. "I wish you two would talk a little."

"We've got to start some kind of work on this exit from hyper-space problem. Maybe we can solve it before it comes time to come out into normal space?"

"There are two other ships . . . out *there* somewhere," Dunn said, "and they probably know what we know by now. Maybe . . . we'll not be the ship which gets through?"

"Shut up, both of you," Hoyt said without looking up. "I'll have no panic on my ship."

Dunn turned to him and said, "I only meant to—"

Hoyt suddenly threw his knife and fork into his plate and stood up, pushing his chair back noisily.

"Everybody, relax," Rescher said. "Please sit down, Captain."

"Look," Dunn said, eager to inject a hopeful note into the scene, "the whole mess revolves around what we know and don't know about hyper-space *and* the ship's drive. For example, how the hell does it know exactly where to go in hyper-space?"

Rescher looked up at Hoyt, who seemed to be looking down at them as if in mockery. Then the tall man sat down, seemingly calmer, and resumed eating.

"I'm going to get some answers, good answers," Dunn said, "because we have to have them." Rescher thought he detected a note of hysteria in the young man's words, but he knew that they would all have to convince themselves, each in his own way, of some kind of hope. He was certain that Jay was thinking off the top of his head. What he was saying seemed hopelessly vague, and probably all wrong.

"Go on," Hoyt said, calm now.

"Well—for starters we can set up a hyper-spatial chamber and try to determine the properties inside. You know, the space inside, whatever it is."

"I don't recommend it; it's dangerous aboard ship," Hoyt said. "You know what Frank said about triggering anomalies. I won't order you to do it."

"It's trying something which might work . . . or spend the rest of our lives aboard this tombship," said Rescher.

Hoyt nodded reluctantly. "Get on it, then."

"I know that tinkering is easy," Dunn said. "I'll be careful, Captain. I only hope that we have the know-how aboard this ship to interpret what results I get to make some sense."

Dunn's chamber was a fistful of gray nothingness on the lab table, enclosed in a clear alloy the shape of a foot square box. Inside it the ship's drive field did not apply, thus permitting the outer-space from outside the hull to spill into the restricted chamber. Rescher watched the box with Dunn. The light trained on the table in the lab was very bright.

"I don't see what this tells us," Dunn said. "Hoyt will be disappointed."

"I keep expecting it to move around in there," Rescher said, "like smoke, you know. But it only sits. And still I get the feeling that it's something *tangible*."

Hopelessness was a gnawing thing in his belly which he had not been able to shake. Maybe he should go back into long-sleep, and when he woke up again for his fourth watch the problem would be solved. He hated to see even Jay's normal optimism shaken. It would all be fixed when he wakened the next time. New worlds would be there for the taking by the eighth watch, and all he would have to do would be to reach out . . . he remembered the long-haired woman he had seen laughing at him from the lounge screen.

"Look!" Dunn said. "Look at that."

In the gray murk of the chamber the woman was smiling at them. Her entire body was visible this time, a beautiful long-legged form, luxurious in thigh and breast; her hair reached to her waist, and it drifted around her as she turned and tumbled slowly in the gray field. Rescher was almost certain it was the same girl.

Suddenly she was no longer naked; she was blonde now and wearing a silver bikini.

"I like dark-haired girls," Rescher said.

And again her hair was dark, but flecked with dazzles of red this time.

"We did *that*," Dunn said. "I like blondes. But how in all hell?"

Near the door the screen intercom buzzed.

Rescher walked over, flicked the switch and watched Hoyt's face appear on the screen.

"Both of you get up to the control area. I've just turned off the simulated tie-in with normal space."

In a moment they were both out in the hallway and walking toward the elevator.

"I know he has the authority," Dunn said, "but I wish he'd told us."

Rescher imagined that the Captain might have been brooding about the truth of what it was like outside the ship. Perhaps he had been displeased with himself for accepting the lie of the screens?

When they came into the control area, Captain Hoyt was sitting in the central command station, staring into the gray murk on the forward screen. All the screens showed the same view. Rescher and Dunn walked up to the seated figure and stood at his right hand. He did not look at them, but continued staring into the screen, seemingly shaken and overwhelmed by this great fact of nothingness.

"It is true, it's all true. I convinced the computer to break the circuit between itself, the black box below and the screens," Hoyt said. "Watch . . . what happens every time." Rescher noted that there was little strength in his voice, as if something had been taken out of him, some personal pride in his relation to reality.

Before them on the forward screen . . . things . . . began to appear out of the great void. Worlds rushed out of the grayness toward the ship, rich green worlds, and orange-yellow suns to warm them, vivid against the gray spaces. They seemed to burst into the nothingness; one moment they were infinitesimal points, the next huge physical bodies.

Rescher saw Hoyt grip the armrests of his command seat. He watched as the strange light from the screen played upon the Captain's tense features.

Now suddenly the space before them was a green vortex of vines and vegetation, a virgin green forest, a great mass floating in other-space.

The ship plowed into it and kept going.

"You two see it?" Hoyt asked. He turned to Rescher and repeated his question. "Frank, you see it, don't you?"

"I see it," Rescher said. Hoyt tried not to look at him directly, Rescher noticed.

"Is it real, can it be *real?*"

"It's as real as whatever real means," Rescher said. He noticed that Hoyt's hands were shaking a bit as he gripped his armrests.

The ship burst out of the green mass of vines and floating plants, and the gray space ahead was now laced with the darkness of normal space, running in with the fluid gray like a mixture of liquid plastics. An eternity away a few stars seemed to twinkle.

"Captain, get a grip on yourself," Dunn said. "You can . . . try and make it go away!" Hoyt ignored Dunn's sudden outburst. At another time he would have received a careful comment on how to address a commanding officer.

Hoyt closed his eyes and his tall frame seemed to hunch over in the chair. He was breathing heavily and shifting his body around now, like a man possessed.

On all four screens in the control room the new worlds continued to appear out of the grayness, heralds of a new cosmos. They seemed to originate from one point and move outward to fill the emptiness. If they are ours, Rescher thought, we reach out with our hunger, create with our hope . . .

"Captain!" Dunn was shouting.

"I can't," Hoyt said. He sat up and opened his eyes.

Rescher thought: *we cannot 'just create' anything. The power which our minds control moves within a given set of structures, categories according to which we think. Our ability should seem no more fantastic than the use of nuclear power, or the harnessing of any new force.* A doubt crossed his mind: *there might easily be an absolute chaos outside our minds, but we select and order and arrange from it to produce order for us. It might be a different order for an alien being. Sometimes it seems different for other people . . . how much order is out there and how much is ours,* he wondered.

On the screens the worlds were gems swimming in a gray-black ocean, rushing past the ship as it came upon them at unimaginable speed; it was the first indication of motion in the new continuum, the first possibilities of space and order within that other-space. *It is a* tangible *thing,* Rescher thought, *not a sterile desert useful only for swift passage from point to point in another universe. Reality abides here also,* and the possibility of it welled up inside him. It was the age-long conviction of all intelligent life, the basis of all achievement and struggle— that here there will be something, and not nothing.

"It seems to be acquiring its own permanence," Dunn said. "It won't change or go away like the girl in the lab."

Hoyt turned in his chair and looked up at Rescher, while Dunn continued to stare at the forward screen, overcome by his own conclusion. "I made those worlds," Hoyt said slowly. "I was sitting here after I turned off the tie-in. I knew we were all doomed, all those below and those still to be born. Failure was in the cards for me if we could not exit from this gray wasteland—and then it began happening, Frank, I could not decide whether it was a good or bad thing." Hoyt covered his face with his hand and Rescher knew that something inside the man had broken. He looked away from him to the forward screen, a petty kindness to the tall man huddled in the command chair.

In Rescher's mind some of the pieces began to fall into place. The solar system anomaly, the recent events on and outside the ship and Hoyt's words—these seemed to link up in a patchwork, which when supported by further events, would fuse into a finished explanation. He looked at Dunn, and he was sure that the younger man was pacing him with his own reasonings as he watched the forward screen. Later, the main computer would help them consolidate all their findings. One element seemed to be lacking from his rough scheme: the *power,* the force which could shape the hyper-spatial stuff into anything, where did it come from? Was it everywhere around them? He knew that his mind could *use* it, but where was the source?

He told Dunn what he thought. Hoyt seemed to be recovering his composure.

"Sure," Dunn said, "agreed. But *how* in hell?" A moment of silence. "The computer will vomit when we try to feed it all this kind of stuff. We'll have to be careful."

IV

"The computer now knows everything we knew about hyperspace on earth," Dunn said, "and what we've learned here and in the ship's lab. We might get a first approximation answer. I've tried to program the computer for extreme flexibility by removing certain kinds of conceptual biases. I've tried to weight its operations toward the use of the group of abilities we call imagination. I'm going to try it now."

Slowly he punched the keys. The three men sat in their command stations in front of the console and waited. Only the forward screen was on, showing the forward rush of the starship into what seemed more densely star-filled space. Rescher was worried about the Captain, who seemed content to let Dunn and himself handle things. He seemed withdrawn, fearful of any reality which seemed impermanent, Rescher thought. All his life the Captain had counted on the fact of a reality beyond himself unchanging and dependable.

The sing-song of the computer at work echoed in the hard acoustics of the control room. In five minutes the waiting was over, and the computer began spewing out its results, in a compact printed type, indicating that there would be a good amount of material. They each started to read their copy, which came out on rolled paper into their laps.

Hypothesis: the term hyper-space refers to a highly plastic substance or potential which exists in a free state outside the various possible universes. Historical scientific thought postulated it as an unformed potential, the substratum of reality.

Hypothesis: this substance or potential seems to be affected by the thinking of the intelligent entities. A few of the discontinuous bodies which have appeared on the ship's screens are such mind-dependent creations; but until now they have been unconscious, lacking in continuity.

It is certain that the solar anomaly was caused by the unleashing of sub-space potentials into normally formed space-time; the immediate cause was the experimentation directed toward the development of a hyper-spatial drive. Space around the sun was affected by the spill-over caused by such experimentation. Various rival human theorizings about the nature of the universe thus vied to become concrete and destroyed the permanence of previously familiar reality: the competition of an indefinite range of human beliefs, from superstition to the problematical areas of modern physics, resulted in the chaotic discontinuity which we refer to as the solar anomaly.
The previous continuum, if it still exists, cannot be entered again without complete destruction of the object attempting it. As the laws within the solar system grow even more inconsistent, the entire grouping of bodies will contract to an infinitesimal point and disappear.

Observation: in the unformed potential around this ship a new cosmos is taking shape. Steps must be taken to direct it consciously before it takes on permanence. Complete consistency is impossible, and undesirable, since it would result in a static creation lacking in variety and the capacity for change and development. The plasticity of the basic materials of reality is the ultimate scientific description. An explanation of this first fact seems to rest on a principle outside the system, not open to proof or examination, but clearly true.

Fact: once a matrix is forged it becomes independent of its efficient creators—minds—and takes on an existence of its own. The beginning must be sufficient to insure that laws which later become apparent will not seem

binding and arbitrary. However, openness is bought with
the inevitability of the final and necessary inconsistency,
which previously was known as entropic decline.

Fact: each of the three ships which left the solar system
is now the center of its own continuum; each new universe is expanding rapidly, and shortly they may impinge
on one another. The effect of the radical adjustment
which will occur then cannot be predicted...

Rescher let the tissue thin paper unroll to the floor. The
earth, the sun, they became real in a vast desert of unreality—
and now the desert had taken it all back. And it would do so
again and again. An eternal creation would be impossible, too
binding and static. Complete knowledge, exhaustive explanation at the basic level, was impossible. Too little knowledge
could be frustrating; too much a bore. Powerlessness would be
pathetic, but omnipotence would exclude accomplishment. What
was left? Something like this—a life which left existence its
mystery, pain its warning sting, pleasure its delights, mind the
fulfillment of its curiosity. Only a certain kind of being can
have these things. A god couldn't, nor could an animal. When
human beings pressed the limits, they lost their individual kind
of being; the precarious balance of mortality and finitude was
precious, the source of that share of glory that was theirs.

Rescher watched Dunn finish reading the printout. The young
man got up from his station seat. Rescher watched him bite
his lower lip, and drop the roll of paper hanging out of the
computer.

"Jay," Rescher said, "you know, there must have been gods,
at some other beginning a long time ago."

"I would like to know," Hoyt said coldly, "how our puny
minds can direct all these forces?"

Immediately Dunn seemed to resent the Captain's critical
tone of voice. "We've been directing forces in one way or
another throughout our whole history, Captain. Think of all
this potential as sitting at the top of a large hill precariously.
Our minds give a push and the show starts. Only a small push
is needed. We've been doing that since the wheel, in some

sense, and the hyper-drive research on earth is another example—and another what we three are doing now."

"If the fields surrounding the other two ships combine with ours, then will we be able to communicate with them?" Hoyt asked.

"Maybe," Dunn said. "They might be trapped in their own cosmos."

"Trapped..." Hoyt stared at the floor plates at his feet.

"I guess," Rescher said, trying to break the Captain's mood, "that Captain Hoyt will contribute to the pessimistic aspects of our next world." He grinned weakly at Dunn, who shrugged.

But Hoyt looked up at them suddenly and shouted, "Damn both of you! The devil knows what will happen—maybe we are all insane, did you think of that?"

"Take it easy, Captain," Rescher said. For a moment he felt the unreality of the whole scene. He didn't trust his senses, or his sanity. A moment of terror passed through him, like a cold knife slowly being drawn through his guts. He thought of all those asleep in the central hold of the ship. And he remembered that they could not dream. Their sleep state was deep, deliberately induced and maintained to avoid dreams. A man could suffer, even in a dream; every possible way to mark time had been taken from the sleepers. He shuddered at the impossible thought of what their unrestrained dreaming might have done in the present situation, the contortions reality might have been subjected to if their thoughts had been able to reach out from their sleeping forms. Perhaps in a small way some of their thoughts were trickling out?

He turned to say something to his troubled Captain...

And faced an ocean. On the far horizon it touched an azure sky, cloudless, solid in color. Below the dune he stood on, the breakers rolled in gently from the sparkling green sea.

He was afraid. A strong mind could completely sweep away the reality of a weaker mind; control probability according to its designs; become god for a host of lesser minds. In an unjust creation this might all be possible. Who had done *this* to him?

Or was this merely himself?

He closed his eyes and tried to visualize the control room on the starship, the floorplates, the computer console with its myriad lights, the giant screens on the four walls...

She came up behind him on the dune and locked her arms around his waist. He wrenched himself free.

"Rita!"

Her eyes looked up at him invitingly from where she lay on the sand. She was so much more vivid, more sensual, than he had remembered.

"You're on the other ship," he said. And he knew with a sadness that it was not her, only his dream of her. This Rita was too willing, too ready for him. This was his world, and he knew that he could not let it go on.

But she persisted. She got up from the sand and came to him and said, "Oh Frank, I miss the exertion of it with you!" She folded herself into his arms like a child and put her cheek against his chest.

He held her briefly, then pushed her away. He had to end it, unless he wanted to talk only to himself and leave other *persons* out of it; most of the reasons for living demanded that there be other people, other minds. He was suddenly afraid of Hoyt. The temptation was great, and he knew what the other man must be struggling with. He gathered his will. It would have to be a public universe, to make any sense. The three of them would have to will it so, and make provision for others to enter it later on. He hoped that the officers on the two other starships felt the same way, or he would never see Rita again. When the three expanding fields met, what would happen then? And when would they meet?

"I suppose it is possible for the three realities—one for each ship—to integrate," Dunn was saying. "And in that case we would be able to communicate with them. But there is no reason to think that it will necessarily happen, Captain."

Rescher was back in the control room. Had he ever left it? Captain Hoyt was on his feet, standing next to Jay. Both men were looking at the active forward screen, waiting.

Rescher was glad that he had broken the continuity of his dream, insuring that it would not become permanent. He was glad to be sharing a reality with Dunn and Hoyt again. Silently he went over to where they stood and joined their watch. A sense of comradeship became their reality as they watched the screen, and Rescher knew that each had faced the same temptation . . . and had resisted.

They watched the screen in silence, watched the new bodies rushing past them, knowing that their bubble of reality was expanding and would perhaps meet with two others. Would the others be radically different? Rescher wondered what he would feel when the time came. A man continued to function because his mind struck a balance between order and chaos, between the known and unknown; if sanity prevailed in the other two ships then the new cosmology would be acceptable. Each of the other six movers, the waking officers aboard the other starships, were educated, trained men with similar outlooks. How much conflict of probabilities would there be when the expanding bubbles met? As much conflict as there normally is among human beings, he told himself. But still, perhaps each bubble *had* to be an individual cosmos . . . and could they ever merge?

Human minds, souls—any word would do—were now the only objectively certain facts besides the flux-like nature of the unformed plenitude which could become an infinity of possible worlds; and human minds would inevitably choose a certain range of possibilities. Wouldn't they?

What if each other ship chose a totally personal universe?

He would never see Rita again . . .

The mind was a fairly constant thing, he told himself, a source of order and directing capacity; about them was the irrational, which here and there in the multi-dimensional stretches of infinite gray "stuff," the mind would succeed in shaping for a time and setting upon a course. The ruling principle of any viable cosmos was evolutionary, but not only in the sense of strict derivation of one thing from the thing coming before it, but also in the possibility of discontinuity, unpredictable emergence: novelty, true creation. He felt uncertain again. If this essentially irrational possibility was stifled no change would be possible; and yet if this possibility were stronger than stability, anomalies of a serious order would set in, playing havoc with physical regularities and ending with the total cancellation of the continuum.

What is needed, Rescher thought as he watched the screen,

is the attitude that our universe might just *become* the best of all possible worlds, but never be certain about it. This kind of thinking might just provide the open sequence of combinations which would produce new things without end, thus avoiding the boredom of certainty and the chaos of uncertainty.

"Hey, Frank." Dunn nodged him with his arm. "I think the computer may have something for us." They both looked at Hoyt. The Captain's face was strangely drawn as he stared at the screen, as if a shadow had been drawn across his face.

The computer sang what seemed to Rescher a row of twelve notes, and said:

PROBABLE NATURE OF EMERGENT CONTIN-UUM EVOLUTIONARY MATTER ENERGY DIS-TINCT EXPANDING SPATIAL DISTRIBUTION OF MATTER   STAR-PLANET-GALAXY-METAGAL-AXY GROUPINGS SEQUENCE INORGANIC-OR-GANIC-EPIORGANIC EXPANSION-CONTRACTION AND EVOLUTIONARY TIME SCALES CANNOT BE DETERMINED AT PRESENT

Briefly, Rescher thought of old Sol, discarded now like an empty nautilus shell when its living center has fled. Perhaps it would be washed up somewhere.

The computer said:

TIME OF MAXIMUM INDETERMINACY IMMI-NENT.

The darkness was complete.

The handprint in the cement was being made.

But whose?

In his aloneness Rescher thought he heard the screams of all the possible creations which had now been excluded. Were the other ships and Rita forever beyond him now?

Why the darkness?

Deep inside himself he felt a shuddering, a shaking, as if a great mass had slammed into him. Space became white, then black in a rapid sequence of black-white-black-white-black-white-black-white . . . A question came and its meaning terri-

fied him . . . blackness buried him . . . white blinded him . . . but
he knew he would have to give an answer before the darkness
could claim him for itself, and he would spend eternity in its
embrace.

Why should there be anything?

Why should there be not only . . . nothing?

Rescher screamed his defiance, as the darkness crept into
his being and caressed him.

He hated it.

Because it wanted to keep him from Rita, from his future,
from the sight of his sons and daughters, from the feel of clean
air in his lungs, the sight of sky and sea. There was only one
answer to the darkness which could ever work.

It is my will that there be something.

He imagined he saw three bubbles of force merge, and the
great edge of reality fled from him like the skin of an expanding
balloon, growing larger with infinite speed. He felt a rocking
motion, a tearing, the inner-outer sensation of three realities
trying to merge, and failing. Three bubbles of force pushing
at each other like three Portuguese Men-of-War trying to become one, three jellyfish trying to absorb one another, and at
last failing, content now to be together but still distinct: three
precious stones in the same setting, they would never be one.

The screens in the control room were lit with the splendor of
vast starfields, of stars very close together, some perhaps only
a light-year apart. Rescher looked at the color filled expanse
and a great surge of emotion swept through him. This was what
they had aimed for when they had left the stricken solar system:
the dream made real. Here would be born a civilization which
would easily span a thousand worlds.

"Frank, come here," Dunn said sharply.

He turned to look at him kneeling beside Captain Hoyt on
the floor.

"He's dead!"

Rescher took a step and knelt next to Dunn. Hoyt's eyes
were still open, staring into the darkness to which he had not
been able to give an answer; the action of a prideful man who
in the end had been unable to believe that so much depended
on his will. The authority of reality had always come to him

from *outside* himself, the strictures of duty and so-called hard facts. The fact was pale, as if a shadow was draped over it. On earth he had left no one, and there was no one for him on any of the other ships.

Dunn reached over and closed the eyes, and touched him affectionately on the right shoulder. Then he stood up. "Do you think we can raise one of the other ships? Will it be possible?"

Rescher looked up at him briefly. The man was looking for something to do, to avoid revealing the tears in his eyes.

"Hey, Frank," Dunn said, "all the stiffs below, they've slept through the Creation. What are we going to tell them?" And he went off toward the main control console by the forward screen.

Rescher stood up and looked down at the body of Hoyt, who had stopped . . . living. His huge frame seemed a bit too small for his green overalls.

He looked up at the forward screen. It would be a *common* universe after all. At least for Dunn and himself and all those who would waken to see it. They would be talking with the other two ships soon . . .

And he would see Rita. But would she be the same? Even if the three bubbles had not merged, there would be a Rita and there would be two other ships. His mind had seen to that. She would be *a* Rita, permanent now despite himself. In time perhaps her personality might diverge from the original who existed somewhere in one of the two other universes—he would love her just the same.

And doubt her.

Elsewhere the *real* Rita might have her version of himself; would she doubt him?

Everything in all three universes, he thought, would be just a bit off. Lovers would be just a little too much like what each expected, but perhaps that wasn't such a bad idea. But again, he reminded himself, everyone would begin to diverge after the creation, and would become different.

At least there would *be* other people, real people. What did a man really want but the happiness of those he loved? Growth; a little bit of difference, a lot of the familiar, the unexpected, the effectiveness of one's will, mystery and a little more than he could ever know. A man could be a small divinity in his own realm. Poised between the infinity of the large and small he could grasp both.

Almost.

He would share the unfolding variety of myriad things with other minds, companions who like himself were interlocking faces of diamonds set in the fabric of eternity.

The Word Sweep

THE words on the floor were as thick as leaves when Felix came into the party. At five past eleven, the room should have been silent.

"Quiet!" he shouted, unable to hold back.

The word formed in the air and floated to the floor at his feet. A deaf couple in the corner continued talking with their hands. Everyone was looking at him, and he felt his stomach tighten. He should have motioned for silence instead of speaking.

A small woman with large brown eyes came up to him and handed him a drink. He sipped. Vodka. It was her way of saying, yeah, we know you've got a lousy job policing the yak ration. Pooping parties for a living can't be fun, you poor bastard. We know.

Heads nodded to show approval of the woman's gesture.

Felix tried to smile, feeling ashamed for losing control. Then he turned and went out again into the cool October night.

At the end of the block, the compactor was waiting for the sweeps to clean out the corner house. He was glad that he did not have to work in the inner city, where control was always slipping, where the babbling often buried entire neighborhoods to a depth of four or five feet.

He took a deep breath. Watching out for five suburban blocks was not so bad, especially when his beat was changed once a month, so he could not grow too friendly with the homeowners.

The tension in his gut lessened. At least this party had not given him any trouble. He could see that the guests had tried to be sedate, speaking as little as possible during the evening, priding themselves on their ability to hold words and liquor. He had not seen any babblers sitting on a pile of verbiage. This was a good block, much better than last month's section.

A dog ran by in the empty street. Felix noted the muzzle. No problem there.

He started a slow walk home, passing the compactor as it turned on its light and started silently down the next block. Two streets down, he turned to avoid going through the district square, where they were still cleaning up after the political rally.

There was a message for him on the phone screen:

> Let's ration together after
> you get home. I'll save
> mine. Love, June

The words angered him, bringing back the tension in his stomach. He cleared the screen, resenting the message because it had ruined the calming effect of his long walk home.

He went into the bedroom and lay down. When he tried, he could almost remember the time when words did not materialize. He must have been four or five when it happened for the first time. He remembered wafer-thin objects, letters joined together in as many differing styles as there were speakers.

At first it had been a novelty, then a perpetual snowstorm. Cities had to clean up after a daily disaster, three hundred and sixty-five days a year, trucking the words to incinerators and landfills. The words would burn only at high temperatures, and even then they would give off a toxic gas which had to be contained. There had been a project to find a use for the gas, but it took too much energy for the burning to make it worthwhile; later the gas was found to be useless.

Psychiatric treatment came to a halt, then shifted to computer printout and nonverbal therapies. Movies had gone back to silent and subtitled versions; only the very rich could afford to truck away the refuse after each talkie showing. Opera was performed in mime and music-only reductions. . . .

Felix opened his eyes and sat up in the darkness. Somewhere far away, a deviant was running through the streets. He could just barely hear the screaming, but it was loud enough to remind him of the time he had been a deviant.

Unable to control himself, he had almost buried himself in words one night, under a giant elm tree near the edge of town. The words had poured out of him as if they were trying to outnumber the stars, while he had held his stomach and screamed obscenities.

Bruno Black, who had been fully grown before the world had changed, had explained it to him later. It had been the silence, the prolonged, thought-filled silence that had broken his control, as it had broken the resolve of countless others. The need to speak had come uncontrollably into him one day, ridding him of cogency, sweeping through him like a wind, bestowing the freedom of babble, taking away wit and limit, making his mouth into a river, out of which words had flowed like wars . . . in the end a wonderful nonsense had cleansed his brain.

Now, as he listened to the distant deviant howling in the night, he again felt the trial of terse expression; the jungle was growing in around him, threatening to wipe away all his control when he fell asleep, enticing him with pleasures stronger than the silence. . . .

He looked around the dark room. The closed bedroom door stood in the corner, a sly construction, suggesting an entire world on the other side. . . .

The distant sound stopped. They had caught him. Samson, Winkle, Blake—all the block watchers had converged on the explosion to squash it. The word sweeps were already clearing up, compacting, driving away to the landfills.

For a moment he wondered if it might have been Bruno, then rejected the idea; Bruno's voice was much lower than that. It might have been a woman.

Felix relaxed and lay back again.

• • •

He woke up in the night, got up and went to his desk. He saw the phone screen glowing and remembered June's message. The new message read:

> You bastard! Answer for
> Christ's sake. Is Bruno
> with you again? What
> do you two do together?

He cleared the screen and turned on the desk lamp. Then he sat down and took out Bruno's journal. He looked at it under the light, remembering how much relief it had given him through the years. His fingers were shaking. Inside its pages were all the things he had wanted to say, but Bruno had written them down.

Opening at random, he looked at the neat handwriting. Bruno was not verbose, even on paper, where it would have been harmless. The very letters were well-formed, the sentences thoughtful and clear. If read out loud, they would not exceed anyone's daily ration.

He read an early entry:

23 July 1941
When the words started materializing, the difference between language and physical reality was blurred. The appearance of spoken words in all shapes and sizes, depending on the articulation of the speaker, imposed a martial law of silence, enforced at first by a quietly administered death penalty in some parts of the world. The rate of materialization had to be cut down at all costs, lest the world be thrown into a global economic depression. . . .

The depression had come and gone, leaving behind a new code of conduct, the word sweeps, the compactors, and the block watchers—and a mystery as great as the very fact of existence. Bruno was certain that there had to be an answer; his journal represented twenty years of speculation about the problem. The possibility of an answer, Felix thought, is all that keeps me together. I don't know what I'll do if Bruno doesn't come back.

Someone started pounding on the front door. Felix got up and went out to check.

He opened the door and June came in, marching past him into the living room, where she turned on the lights.

He closed the door and faced her.

"You treat me like I don't exist!" she shouted.

The *you* was a flimsy thing; it broke into letters when it hit the carpet. *Treat* seemed to be linked like a chain as it clattered onto the coffee table, where it produced a few nonsense-masses before it lay still. *Me* whipped by him like a sparrow and crunched against the wall, creating more nonsense-masses. *Like* settled slowly to the rug; *I* knifed into the pile next to it. *Don't* and *exist* collided in midair, scattering their letters.

Felix spread his hands, afraid to speak, fearful that at any moment his deviancy would slide up out of the darkness within him and take over. Didn't she know how hard a life he led? He'd told her a hundred times. A look of pity started to form on her freckled face, reminding him of the brown-eyed woman who had given him a drink; but it died suddenly. June turned and started for the door.

"We're finished!" she shouted as she went out. The words failed to clear the door as she slammed it behind her, and dropped next to the coat rack. He looked at the nonsense-masses that her pounding had created, grateful that the door was well-cushioned.

He let out a mental sigh and sat down in the armchair by the lamp. At least there would be no more pressure, however much he missed her. Soon, he knew, he would have to go looking for Bruno.

The clock over the fireplace read four A.M.

He turned on the radio and listened to the merciful music. The notes formed, evaporating one by one. A harpsichord came on, the notes lasting a bit longer before winking out. He watched them come and go for a long time, wondering, as Bruno had done so often in his journal, what kind of cosmic justice had permitted music to remain. As the Scarlatti sonata rushed toward its finale, the crystalline sounds came faster and faster, dusting the room with vibrant notes. . . .

June had never liked Bruno; there was no darkness in her. Like those who were forgetting the self-awareness created by speech, she did not need to speak.

He turned off the radio and wondered if Mr. Seligman next door was burying himself in sleeptalk. How many children were sleeping with their training muzzles on, until they learned self-control?

His hands started shaking again. The pressure to speak was building up inside him, almost as strongly as during his deviant days. June's visit had triggered it; the loss of her had affected him more than he realized.

"June," he said softly, wanting her.

The word was round, the letters connected with flowing curves, as it drifted to the rug. He reached down, picked it up and dropped it into the felt-lined waste basket.

His hands were still shaking. He got up and paced back and forth. After a few minutes he noticed that his screen was on in the bedroom. He walked through the open door, sat down at the desk, and read:

> Disturbance reported at the
> landfill. Check when your shift
> begins this morning. Webber

One of the others has gone nuts, he thought, and they want me to bring him home.

Felix changed his shirt and shoes and went outside. He unlocked the bicycle from its post, mounted the cracked leather seat, and pushed out into the empty street.

Cool, humid mists rose around the one-story suburban houses. Only every fifth streetlamp was on, and these began to wink out as the sky grew brighter. He estimated that it would take him half an hour to reach the landfill.

He remembered it as a plain of dry earth being blown into dust clouds by the wind. The place would soon be incapable of accepting any more words, or garbage; it was full, except for an occasional hole. A new site would have to be found.

As Felix neared the landfill, he noticed the strangeness of the grass on both sides of the road. The sun cleared the horizon in a clear blue sky; and the grass suddenly looked like matted animal hair, growing up from a red skin. There was a pungent, lemon-like odor in the air as he stood up on the bicycle to climb a hill.

He reached the top and stopped.

The landfill was covered with trees, looking like fresh moss, or tall broccoli. The sharp smell was stronger.

He got back on the seat and rolled downhill.

A stillness enveloped him when he reached bottom, as if he had entered the quiet center of the world. As the forest came closer, he considered the possibility of a massive planting program but realized that it would not have been possible in so short a time.

He passed the first trees. They appeared very fresh, like the limbs of young girls, bent upward, open in inviting positions; soft yellow-green moss had grown between the branches.

He pedaled forward, growing anxious, but the stillness was restful, calming him. The lemon-like scent of the trees cleared away the sleepiness in his head.

Suddenly he rolled into a small clearing and stopped short at the edge of a large hole. Bruno Black sat at the bottom, talking to himself as the words piled up around him.

"Hello, Bruno." The words formed and slid down the sandy slope.

The blond-haired man looked up. "Come down." The words popped away from his mouth and landed on the pile.

Felix started down.

"It's safe here," Bruno shouted, "we can talk all we want."

When he reached the large, seated figure, Felix noticed that Bruno's clothes were torn and dirty.

"You've got to let me get you out of this," Felix said.

Only the first three words formed, falling at his feet.

"Notice that?"

"What's going on here, Bruno?"

No words formed this time, as if the effect was beginning to die away.

"It's only here," Bruno said, "nowhere else."

Felix sat down next to the ruddy-faced man and looked at him carefully.

"Bruno—you know me?"

"Of course, Felix, don't be stupid. You're my friend."

"What are you doing here?"

"I think I've figured it—all of it, why it happens, and why it fails here." The last three words formed, wretched little gray letters floating in the air like smoke.

Bruno brushed them away with a bear-like swipe.

"Felix, I may really know. I'm not nuts."

Felix heard a wind rushing above the hole, as if something were growing angry. He remembered a schoolyard, many years ago, with children playing volleyball, silently.

"Have you got a shovel?"

"No," Felix said, "but I can get one."

Again no words. Bruno was watching him.

"Wonderful, isn't it?"

"Bruno—how long has all this been here?"

"About a month."

"All this grew in a month?"

"The trees grew out of the buried words, Felix, pregnant words they were. . . ."

The silence was clear between them, devoid of words.

"It comes and goes," Bruno said. All the words appeared, letters deformed, as if they were gnarly tree branches, and fell into Bruno's lap.

"There's something that does this," he said as he brushed them away. "We can bring it all to an end, when we find it. The shovel is the key to the whole business."

It all made a peculiar sense.

"There's a utility shed at the fork in the road," Felix said, "but are you okay?"

"I just look bad."

There were no words. Felix marveled as he scrambled out of the hole. Bruno was definitely on to something.

Bruno was digging with his hands when Felix came back with two shovels. He threw them in and clambered down.

"It couldn't be natural, what happened to the world," Bruno said as he picked up a shovel and started digging. Felix picked the other one and they dug back-to-back.

"Why not natural?" Felix asked.

"Maybe it could—some twist in the geometry of space

forms words in response to our sounds. I assumed it wasn't natural and went looking for spots where it wouldn't happen."

"Why did it all start?"

"Maybe it was a political thing," Bruno said. "Somebody was planning a form of thought control, but it got out of hand. A while back, I think, our politicos contacted an alien civilization in some far space, a mind contact maybe, and learned how to construct . . . certain devices. Perhaps the alien culture thought it would help us think more concisely." He laughed. "It's more than poetic prankery, you see. Language, as much as toolmaking, is directly responsible for the growth of our intelligence and self-consciousness. We're as smart or stupid as how well we use words. It's the automatic programs, the habits, that deaden the mind, the dogmatic mazes. . . ."

He paused. "Not this hole, we've got to try elsewhere."

Bruno might simply be crazy, Felix thought, nothing more.

"If you wanted to affect a culture," Bruno continued, "put a restriction on its use of language and watch native ingenuity increase, like the improvement of hearing in the blind. . . ."

Felix climbed out of the hole and gave Bruno a hand up.

A wind was blowing across the landfill, soughing through the strange trees as if it were slowly becoming aware of the intruders. Leaves lay strewn everywhere. Some seemed to be stained by decay, like old misshapen coins; others were curling into small tubes. The wind gusted, swirling them into disarray, imparting its energy of motion to raise them into the air. Again Felix had the sensation of standing at the edge of the world. He wondered what June would think if she were to see him here with Bruno.

Then he noticed that the trees seemed to be shaped like letters, bent and distorted, echoing the millions of words buried in the ground.

"Let's dig by one of the trees," Bruno said. The seven words flew out of his mouth and were lifted by the wind, which deposited them in the branches, where they sat like blackbirds.

Felix went up to the nearest tree and started digging. Bruno joined in. The sun climbed toward noon.

"Testing," Bruno said. No word appeared. "Maybe it was something in our minds that was altered, to make the words when we speak. . . ."

"You mean there may be no machine?"

"What's that?" Bruno asked, pointing.

A crystalline rod was protruding from the dirt. Felix stepped into the hole and continued digging while Bruno rested. Slowly, a complex mechanism was uncovered, a cube-like shape of glassy-metallic connections, a maze of shiny pipes and joints, mirror surfaces and solid figures.

"It's . . . like a large piece of jewelry," Felix said.

"I was afraid of this," Bruno said. "I thought there might be a relay device, a generator, the thing that changed speech into solid objects, worldwide, of course, I was hoping to find the local station in the net. . . ."

"Well, what's this then?"

Bruno clutched at his chest and fell forward, easing himself down with the shovel.

"You're ill," Felix said, squatting down next to him.

"My heart . . . but listen. I may die, but you have to listen. . . ."

A demented stare came into Bruno's face, as if he knew that his understanding of the truth was superior to all the deceiving forces around him. He pulled himself backward on the ground, until he was sitting up against the tree, one foot in the hole.

"Try not to move, I'll get help," Felix said.

"Listen!" He raised his hand to his eyes and rubbed them. Then he stared at the alien artifact and spoke, his voice a low, silken tenor. "Humankind fell into a dream. Maybe it was the result of some massive failure, brought on by the straining of psyches long overworked with the yoke of metaphor and simile, paradigm and tautology—in a creature that longed to know the universe directly, tired of sense-show charades, the shadows of real things projected through the dirty windows of the eye, the noisy avenues of the ear. . . ."

His voice grew plaintive and sad. "We grew discouraged by the blindness of touch, the lie of taste and smell, disappointed by the children's universe of not-too-little and not-too-much, of knowing and not knowing, of anxious flight from ignorance into only relative knowledge, stretched tightly between the extremes of sufficiency and insufficiency, between the great and small. We would never be all-knowing, yet we were not *nothing*. The hopelessness was too much, driving us into this common delusion." He closed his eyes and Felix saw tears in his friend's face.

"But maybe it is an alien yoke," Felix said.

"I would prefer that, but this silly machine. . . ."

He coughed and clutched his chest.

"Bruno!"

Felix picked up the shovel and struck the ornate machine. It was a blow for objectivity, forging a way into a universe outside delusion, for an end to the torment of the brute words struggling to break out of him. He hit the machine again; maybe the blow would alter something in the human mind.

"Even if we end this," Bruno whispered loudly, "we don't know what else we may awaken into."

Felix struck the machine a third time.

"It's only a projection of our wish, Felix, to find an answer. . . ."

The world darkened and the wind threw branches onto them and the machine. The device shimmered and disappeared. The branches were like snakes as Felix struggled to free himself. There was a horrible sound from Bruno. Felix crawled toward him and looked into his face. Bruno's eyes were glassy, like the crystal of the machine, staring into an abyss.

"I see it," Bruno croaked, his words trembling.

Felix looked around. A black bag had been pulled down over the world.

"What is it?"

"I see it all!" The words vibrated, but did not form.

"I don't see anything." The blackness was impenetrable.

"Senseless . . . blind, nothing there for us," Bruno muttered.

Felix strained to see. The dark shimmered. He heard a howling in his ears; his eyes rushed forward through a confusion of colors; he expected to collide with a wall at any moment.

"Nothing for us," Bruno was saying, "only constraints, humiliating chains for a will that can expand to infinity or focus into smallness . . ."

The continuum tilted and Felix was falling. Chaos crept into him. Not the sense of chance or statistical disorder obeying its own laws, but mindless, unpredictable fluidity, cruel, unrestrained and unredeemable—the pulsing substratum of reality.

He perceived it in the only way possible, with the narrow gauge of finite senses—a gray, alien mass at the center of time, at the heart of mind, enveloping all space, a cosmic jack-in-the-box always ready to give the lie to all pretense, a centrality which could never be defeated, only held in degrees of check.

"Bruno!" he called, but the word came out as nonsense.

The darkness faded and he saw Bruno sitting up against the tree.

"You're okay!" Felix shouted in relief.

Bruno looked up, but he seemed to be on the other side of a barrier. "Wic wore tos repelton," he said, smiling.

"What?"

"Repelton, tos?"

They stared at each other as the last quantum of information slipped across the bridge of silence, revealing the situation to them.

Felix took a step forward, but Bruno seemed to retreat, as if there were a frame around him and something had moved him back.

Cages, Felix realized. We'll die alone unless we can reach each other. He would never touch June again, or even speak to her; they would look at each other through the wrong end of a telescope, trying to rename the simplest things with gibberish. Our illnesses, our desire to transcend the world, have deformed everything.

Bruno was waving at him. "Tos? Wixwell, mamtom ono!" He shrugged. "Prexel worbout it," he added.

Felix cursed, but the word was indecipherable as two copies appeared and settled to the ground near his feet.

MORE SCIENCE FICTION ADVENTURE!